UNCHIPPED:
KAARINA

UNCHIPPED:
KAARINA

TAYA DEVERE

DVM
PRESS

DVM Press
Vaakunatie 16 D 14
20780 Kaarina, Suomi-Finland
www.dvmpress.com
www.tayadevere.com

This is a work of fiction. Names, characters, places, and incidents either are the products of the author's imagination or are used fictitiously. Any resemblance to actual persons, living or dead, businesses, companies, events, or locales is entirely coincidental.

For information about special discounts available for bulk purchases, sales promotions, fund-raising and educational needs, contact sales@dvmpress.com

ISBN 978-952-7404-02-7 First Ebook Edition
ISBN 978-952-7404-03-4 First Print Edition

Cover Design © 2020 by Deranged Doctor Design -
www.derangeddoctordesign.com
Formatting by Polgarus Studios – www.polgarusstudios.com
Editing by Christopher Scott Thompson and Lindsay Fara Kaplan

To all underdogs out there:
The black sheep, the odd ducks, the rejects, the loners.
You make this world go around.

MIRANDA'S REVENGE

A short story in the world of the Unchipped series

The light of early morning glimmers through the sauna window's tinted glass. Weak sunlight exposes smudges of toothpaste on the bathroom mirror. She reaches for a pill bottle with a small, handwritten X on its label. The dim numbers of a digital clock display are visible in the mirror's upper right corner: 14:08, rather than 7:08 as it ought to say.

The house is quiet, empty apart from Maija. As it has been for nearly fourteen years, since the day her husband stepped into his loafers, clicked open the front door, and half-heartedly called out that he was going to the kiosk to buy a pack of cigarettes.

Sitting by the kitchen window, she had waited a long time for his return. Hours later, after three unanswered phone calls, Maija had found herself in the IT-room, staring at the digital pad of the *Home-Helper* attached to

1

the wall. The blue light of at least twenty icons reflected on her face: glowing images of a camera, dishwasher, shopping bag, showerhead, hair dryer, an envelope, Augmented Reality glasses…

Most of it should work manually, though she wasn't sure. The system had not been shut off since the day it was activated. Not having the AI on—serving and watching over every moment they spent in the house—would have driven Maija's husband mad in a matter of minutes.

She tapped the icon with tools on it.

"Settings — opening", a familiar robotic voice responded after a two second delay.

Maija kept on tapping.

"Home-Helper — shutting down", the voice echoed in the small IT-room for the last time before the system turned itself off with a *whoosh*.

Was she surprised that her husband had left her?

Hardly.

In fact, she'd been waiting for it. The house—their home—had felt meaningless long before he ran away. Their whole lives had felt meaningless actually, ever since the day their daughter had moved out.

The moment the robotic voice fell silent, Maija breathed easier.

Deep down, she hated them both: her runaway husband, and the AI he had named Miranda.

Against all sanity, Maija felt as if the two of them had eloped together: the *Home-Helper* lady and the father of her child.

Fourteen years later, his winter jacket still hangs in the mudroom. There's no sign Miranda was ever here. Or maybe there's something: the dimly lit digital clock, continuously misleading Maija with a false time.

She knows it would make sense to sell the house. She also knows how much of it has gone to pot since she shut down Miranda fourteen years ago. Thanks to her husband's love of modern technology, the house had plenty of digital gadgets—all controlled by Miranda. She didn't even want to think about how much it had cost.

Maija's daughter Kaarina was always reminding her that it was 2088, and that she would do well to join the rest of humanity and live in the present. Just like Maija, she avoided mentioning her father or his disappearance. The two women have talked about him only a handful of times, usually when discussing the oversized house in the middle of the city, and what a joke it was to have only one person living in it.

"Just let me write the ad for you, Mom. And I know, the market's bad right now. But there are *a lot* of suckers out there, still wanting a bigger house than what the Happiness-Program will provide them with. The chip-credits you'd get for this house… You could retire tomorrow."

Kaarina visits for brunch every Sunday morning. The last time she came, she grabbed the tablet from Maija's hands and x-ed out the online newspaper her mother had been reading.

Though reading the news usually does more damage than good to her mental health, Maija still has a hard time looking away. Especially if it has something to do with the *reason* for the bad housing market. It's like a car accident on the side of the road: you have every intention of just driving by, but you can't stop yourself from peeking.

It's depressing. Terrifying. It can't be helped.

The tablet is the only electronic gadget more complicated than a toaster that Maija still uses around the house. Kaarina had finished her last sip of black coffee and set the cup down in the kitchen sink. Her eyes never left the screen. "We can create the listing together. Says right here: 'First thirty days, free of charge.' What do you have to lose, Mom?"

My home. My memories. My dignity.

The words echoed in her mind, but she didn't say them out loud. Instead, she stared at her daughter and wondered when those small wrinkles had appeared around her little girl's forest-green eyes.

"Mom? Mom!"

Maija forced a smile and nodded toward the tablet. "I'll think about it, hon. Now give me that damn thing so I can check the weather. I want to take Ässä out for his walk without getting soaked."

As if responding to her words, the small terrier barked once. Ässä had probably been waiting by his leash near the front door.

Now the pill bottle rattles in her hands. The seal is gone, though Maija hasn't yet taken a single pill out. Maybe she never will.

It'd be easier to go with the flow.

Move with the masses.

Follow orders and join that new Happiness-Program.

Live inside a carefully designed safe box, one that'll soon be fenced in with a stone wall two meters tall.

Her brain sends a signal to her hand, telling it to put the pill bottle back on the bathroom shelf. But much like her technology-hating mind—her hand refuses to obey.

Maija hears a lot about the current state of humanity at the city hospital where she works. It's all they really talk about, the nurses and doctors and IT-people, while sipping their stale coffee drinks in the third-floor break room. The burning topic every day: how there are more people downstairs at the hospital morgue than there are upstairs getting treatment.

"Did you hear, Maija? The population of the U.S. is down eighty percent. First all the mass shootings, and then so many people starving. They're talking about a race war in Europe and about a possible plague in the United Kingdom. Does it get any crazier than this?"

Maija toys with the string of the teabag resting against her mug. After dipping the teabag into hot water, she blows into the cup. A conversation about the violent world is the last thing she wants, but the man talking to her is the chief surgeon. He has never been anything but kind and courteous toward her. Forgiving his inability to read her state of mind comes easily to Maija.

She lifts the mug to her lips, then quickly puts it back down. This hot, the tea would surely burn her mouth. Instead of sipping her tea, she sighs and decides to engage in the conversation. "Not that much better here either."

"How do you mean?"

The teabag dances in the water. "There are not many Finns left either. I think ninety percent of the population can fit inside the city limits now. And with all the stores and services outside of Helsinki shut down, anyone left in the suburbs will soon have no choice but to move here with everyone else."

"That isn't news; I already know all that. What I don't understand is how you can compare our situation in the East with the situation in the West."

She brings the mug back to her lips and carefully takes a tiny sip. The liquid burns her lips, then her throat, but she takes another sip anyway. "People killing themselves is not any better than people killing each other. The Great Affliction is happening everywhere. Just because we have fewer shootings and no wildfires doesn't mean these deaths wouldn't affect us just the same."

"Maybe so, but suicide candidates are easier to treat

than self-styled commandos, running around waving guns at everybody. With the chipping and the Happiness-Program we might be the first nation to recover from this…"

His words fade away as Maija stares at the drowned teabag. She pulls the string to bring the bag back up for a quick breath of air, then watches it slowly sink back to the bottom of the mug.

"Anyway, I'd better get to it. They need extra hands at the morgue today. Might as well make myself useful. When's your chipping again? I didn't see your name on the schedule…"

Eyes locked on her steaming tea, Maija shrugs before answering his question. "I haven't decided if I want the damn thing."

Her colleague stops in the doorway and turns around. "But Maija, you do want to keep your job, don't you?"

She turns to stare at him. Her expression is question enough.

"The chipping is not something for you to think about. Didn't you see latest memo? As of today, it's a mandatory procedure."

The cap on the pill bottle comes off with a *pop*. White pills shaped like tiny American footballs lie at the bottom of the container. With her index finger and thumb, she fishes one of them out the bottle and holds it up to the bathroom light.

So small, so innocent. Escape in a bottle.

Today, she's expected to clock in and walk straight into the hospital's surgery wing. Some of her colleagues will be there as well, getting ready for their brain implants and the better tomorrow it's supposed to bring them all.

Yesterday, Laura Solomon, head of the chipping program, had finally cornered her at the lab, carrying a tablet with a form asking for her medical information. Maija was the only one who hadn't yet signed up for chipping.

Laura had placed the tablet in front of Maija on her desk. "You'll feel absolutely nothing, dear. It's like a quick nap, that's all. You'll get to go home later the same day and come to work the next day, just as if nothing happened. Except that you'll be safe. And fully ready for the Happiness-Program, once it kicks into full swing."

Doctor Solomon gave her the creeps. Always had. Maybe it had something to do with her habit of calling everyone "dear" or "sweetheart," when those people were the same age or older than her. Ever since Solomon's mother, Mrs. Salonen, had stepped back from her role in the company, her daughter seemed to be trying to adopt her leadership style, however awkwardly, even while taking the company in a new direction.

"With the augmented reality, wellness channels, and vegan diet, you'll feel as good as new in no time. We all will. The city will be the most beautiful place to live. Always sunny, always pleasantly warm. My dear, it'll be like we all suddenly live in Malibu."

"What about rain?"

Doctor Solomon cocked her head. "Come again, dear?"

"I understand that the heat-radiating buildings and walkways will melt snow and ice. But what about rain? Does it rain all the time in Malibu during winter months? It sure does here in Finland."

Clearly annoyed by her question, the doctor had cleared her throat and removed an invisible piece of lint from her white coat. "Sweetheart, you won't have to worry about rain—or much of anything else—once you live in the blue city."

Leaning against the bathroom sink, Maija forces herself to think of Kaarina. She closes her fist around the white pill. Her short nails press painfully against her palms.

Kaarina will live in the city.

She'll be chipped, just like everyone else.

It'll be okay, just like Doctor Solomon said.

Maija shakes her head at her thoughts as another voice takes over. It's still her voice—her thoughts—but the message is now less optimistic and positive. More real.

What about Ässä? Will you agree to replace him with a digital dog?

And what, you're going to start calling the drugs they numb you with "happiness pills"? Will you be too afraid to call them what they really are—antidepressants? Just like everyone else?

Do you really believe that perfect weather and a chip in your brain will bring you happiness?

Pressed against her palm, the white pill waits for her to make up her mind. A white pill, much like the happiness pills everyone will soon be taking in the blue city.

But this pill is not part of the Happiness-Program, or the augmented reality the city tenants will soon get to enjoy through their government-issue AR-glasses.

This white pill was not prescribed by Doctor Solomon, but by a nurse gone rogue.

After Doctor Solomon had left the room, silence filled the hospital lab. The machines and other equipment rested quietly in their places, all shut down and useless. Maija stared at the tablet Doctor Solomon had left on her desk. The next available time slot was in just one day. Maija's time had run out.

The lab door opened and closed behind her. Too occupied by her thoughts to check which of her colleagues had walked in, Maija kept staring at the blue light emanating from the device in front of her.

"Having second thoughts, are we?"

The slightly nasal voice belonged to her colleague, Nurse Saarinen.

"Sounds like I don't have that luxury."

"What's that?"

Maija finally looked up from the blank form. The nurse's face was serious but calm.

"Having second thoughts. It's not an option anymore. The chip is mandatory, right? If I want to keep my job?"

Nurse Saarinen's smile didn't reach her eyes. She took a step back and gestured around the empty lab, like she was showing Maija around her workspace for the first time. "Not to state the obvious here…but what job? In case you haven't noticed, none of the patients that arrive to this hospital are breathing. I guess you can still draw their blood and figure out whether it was rat poison or moonshine they used to take their lives."

Maija pushed aside the tablet and crossed her arms on her chest. "So if I'm already out of a job, why is the chipping even necessary?"

"Well, you want to keep living in the city, don't you?"

A shrug was enough to keep the nurse talking.

"Anyone without a chip won't do so well here, not after the augmented reality with its holograms and digital tiles gets up and running. The electricity running through the city, the self-driving vehicles—all of it—will demand a successfully installed brain implant to work.

11

You'll need to be integrated with the Chip System."

"And I'll be what, a part of a computer then?"

"In some sense, I guess you will be. Yes."

"Must be Miranda's revenge..." Maija mumbled and turned back to Doctor Solomon's tablet.

"What's that?"

She reached for the tablet and entered her date of birth into the first empty field. "Nothing."

Nurse Saarinen took a few steps across the space separating them and sat down on Maija's desk. "Why are you so against the chipping? Don't you want humanity to be cured? For these mass suicides to end?"

Maija's hand froze on the tablet. A strong sensation coursed through her. Disgust? Desperation? Rage? Maybe it was all three, bundled together. Maybe she just despised the tablet in front of her, for stripping away her freedom to choose.

Maija stood up, her face only a few inches away from Nurse Saarinen's. Coolness in her voice, she said, "Why? You're asking me *why* I'm not okay with someone else deciding how I'm supposed to spend the rest of my days? *Why* I hesitate at the idea of popping pills every day, when I don't feel suicidal or isolated? Not everyone is doomed to die. Some of us still have something to live for."

"You mean your daughter? I think I saw her appointment on the chipping schedule. Only a few weeks from now."

Kaarina's face flashed through Maija's mind. How

her green eyes lit up with excitement as she described the blue tiles that circle the soon-to-be-lit city. Or the government-provided food service she would then get to use every day. And how she had already sent a job application to the city's Pedal-Center, where people would ride electric bikes to keep the digital society running.

Why can't she join in her daughter's excitement? Why can't she be thrilled about their nation's second chance?

"I still think it's fundamentally wrong. That we can't decide for ourselves." Maija got up and started pacing in circles. "I don't know, maybe I should file a complaint. Talk to people, see if there are others who feel the same way as I do."

Nurse Saarinen's mouth twitched at her words. Her eyes searched Maija's face. Something flickered there, but Maija couldn't read what it was.

Maija walked back to the desk. Her chin held high, she reached for the tablet and pressed the ON/OFF button. The blue light changed to dim gray. "That's what I'll do. I can't be the only one who feels hesitant about becoming Chipped."

Nurse Saarinen stared at her in silence. Her frown revealed some inner battle. Finally, she hopped down from the lab table and walked to a cabinet across the room. With her I.D. card, she popped open a small box inside the metal locker.

She walked back to Maija holding a white pill bottle.

There was a small red X on the label.

"Well…there *is* another way."

The wooden sauna stool seems to drill into her tailbone. She's been sitting there for nearly two hours, holding a white pill—now partly dissolved—between her thumb and index finger—her second chance for what she considers to be a normal life.

She'll still need to go through the operation and get the chip. But with a bit of help from this small drug—and Nurse Saarinen—she won't be turned into some kind of a half-human-half-machine. She'll be something Doctor Solomon calls Unchipped: a person who can't be integrated with the system.

Kaarina will get the house, once she moves into the city. Which should be soon. Blue tiles already decorate the sidewalks of their neighborhood. Everything's nearly ready.

Maija will happily go live somewhere else. In the suburbs, or the woods. Away from technology, brain implants, and alternative realities. Miranda's eerie voice used to give her chills; now the thought of living in an imaginary city with digital plants and animals makes her sick to her stomach.

She won't be lonely. Just like most people these days, dating and friendships aren't something that come to her naturally. At some point they stopped being worth pursuing. Once people got too wary of one another, too afraid to speak out loud in any forum, social media became a thing of the past. By that point, people had been interacting exclusively over smart phones and computers for so many years that talking to each other face to face no longer felt natural.

These gloomy thoughts give her the final push. She claps the pill to her mouth before she can reconsider. She swallows the white pill. A few quick strides take her from the sauna bench to the bathroom sink. A gulp of water flushes down the pill.

She leans against the sink and stares into her own bottle-green eyes, staring back at her in the mirror.

Eat your digital heart out, Miranda…

Smiling, she turns to leave the bathroom. The chipping is in one hour, so she'd better get going.

Just as she reaches for the door handle, the white bathroom tiles around her start to spin. A burning sensation rises from her stomach and travels up toward her throat. Her legs buckle. Her feet go numb.

After a stumbling step backwards, she falls onto the bathroom floor.

Foam dripping from her mouth, her eyes lock on the bathroom mirror and its digital clock. The numbers turn neon-blue, showing her the time: 9:08—as it should be.

"Front door — unlocked."

Miranda's voice seems to come from under water. Even muffled and distant, it still sends cool shivers through Maija's shaking body.

Unhurried footsteps make their way to the bathroom door.

Blinking is hard. Breathing even harder. Her vision blurs as darkness starts to close in.

"Test subject — vital signs low."

The door opens. A pair of white lab shoes stop in front of her cold, sweat-covered face. A woman's hand carefully places a pill bottle into Maija's unmoving palm.

This bottle has a red triangle on its side. Maija's vision is too blurry to read the label, but she knows it by heart.

"Caution. Opioid. Risk of Overdose and Addiction."

Small, colorful pills ripple around her unmoving body. They spread around the white bathroom tiles, some landing in her hair, some rolling under the sauna bench a few feet away.

Just before Maija takes her last breath, she hears a familiar voice speak.

"So sorry about this, dear. Should have kept your thoughts to yourself." The doctor's white coat rustles as she kneels on the floor. With a gentle gesture, she fixes a lock of blonde hair behind Maija's ear. "People like you are simply too dangerous to keep around."

1

KAARINA

November 2088
East-Land, City of Finland

CHAPTER 1
THE WOODS

The silver duct tape wrapped around her worn-out sneaker snaps in half. A cold burst of muddy water fills her shoe, soaking her torn Nordic boot sock from toe to heel. Pushing up the narrow brim of her wool hat, she peeks at the sky. A gray, dreary blanket of clouds rests above her head. The forest is quiet, still. She has about two hours, maybe three, until the dusk arrives.

"That's okay. Just keep going," Kaarina says to herself. Stopping won't do. She should just walk on, ignoring the unpleasant sensation that her toes are swimming in yesterday's heavy rain.

Two more steps forward and the wetness reaches her ankle. Cursing under her breath, Kaarina stops and sits on a moss-covered rock under the pine trees that rise above her, motionless and somber, just like the clouds above the treetops.

"You just couldn't keep it together, then? For one more day?" Like a madwoman, she holds the ragged sneaker at eye level and points at it, as if the damn shoe were to blame for the current state of her life.

After glaring and cursing at it for a minute, she drops the shoe on the ground. With a dull *thump* it lands next to her, the strip of duct tape still attached: useless but holding on. She sits on the rock with legs folded beneath her, arms wrapped around her knitted legwarmers. Her backside aches slightly as it presses against the harsh surface.

It's unnaturally warm, too humid for November. Drops of sweat trickle down her ribcage beneath her navy-blue hoodie. Too bad her winter gear is the most presentable attire she owns. Otherwise she would have worn her shredded jeans and the long-sleeved black T-shirt, the one with a horse head silhouette printed on its ripped chest pocket. Her favorite clothes, regardless of the white stains under the armpits, or the fact that if she were to bend over in those timeworn jeans, her equally ragged underwear would see daylight.

She'd get new clothes, eventually. New hair too. Should she keep her short blond hair? Or maybe long, brown curls would be nice for a change. She'll decide on her new identity later. Once she moves back to the city.

Her improvised seat is no longer so uncomfortable now that the hard granite has made her numb. The sleepy forest surrounding her feels tranquil and static, like every branch and leaf and plant has frozen solid overnight. But they've yet to witness the first frost of fall. If the horses, dogs, cats, and rabbits that visit the barn weren't shedding madly, she'd guess Mother Nature was planning to skip winter altogether this year.

A low rumble from her stomach breaks the uncanny silence. Did she forget to eat this morning, before she started this hopeful hike toward the city? An image of two crispbreads topped with cowberries flashes through her mind. No—she didn't skip lunch after all. Or was it yesterday's breakfast she's thinking of? Or last night's supper?

She scans the damp forest floor. Pine and spruce needles mingle with half-burned debris: stained and torn plastic bags, a disposable raincoat, a damaged bucket, mismatched gardening gloves, a white IKEA writing desk. Five, ten, and fifty-Euro bills poke out from the pile of abandoned belongings, moldering in the wet ground. She's seen birds collecting them. They use the now worthless notes to build their nests in the spring.

About ten meters further on, another dump filled with random detritus rises from the underbrush: more things that no longer have any value. Not after their owners did their best to burn it all, before hurrying to their new lives in the buzzing city.

In the distance, streetlights flicker on. It's too early, but the gloom of the day has fooled the automatic sensors into thinking it's already nighttime.

A muffled sound echoes through the woods— someone hollering a child's name. It makes Kaarina wish there was another path. An alternative route that she could use to travel deeper in the woods and further away from this dump that used to be the suburbs.

"Girl, you gotta find yourself a new pair of shoes."

Kaarina reaches for the worn-out sneaker on the ground to closer investigate the damage. She rips off the half-attached duct tape and tosses it next to a burned teddy bear with one button eye. "Great idea Bill, thanks for that. I'll add it to my shopping list, right after my new down jacket and a pair of un-holy socks."

She pulls the now-tapeless shoe back on, grimacing when mud gushes between her toes. Continuing her journey is a must—she needs to get to the city and back before dark. Unsure whether she's gathering her mind or her body, Kaarina sits still and stares at her shoes, one still held together with silver duct tape, one showing off her mud-soaked blue-green sock.

"It's not a real word."

"What isn't?"

"Un-holy. Not a word. And is that manure that covers your so-called footwear? Christ on a crutch, Kay… I know things are bad but come on!"

Just like the wet sludge in her shoe, she pretends the voice in her head isn't there. That she isn't here. Alone in the woods beneath a ceiling of gray clouds, surrounded by damp surfaces and endless rows of mushrooms. Instead of coming up with a witty response, something to get Bill off her back, she counts the rows of chanterelles, milkcaps, and yellowfoots. *Sixteen… twenty-nine…thirty-two.* There are enough of them to feed a village. But there's no village left for her to feed.

"Aren't you getting sick of eating those things? Would it kill you to eat some meat? In case you haven't noticed, it's challenging to score vegan-points when most people around you are long dead or have all gone rogue."

"I'll stop by at the shop on my way back."

"The small one by the brook? It's empty, remember? Nothing left but free buckets and lottery tickets. Maybe you can catch a rat or two. Make some casserole."

"I haven't had meat since I turned twelve. And I'm not about to start eating it now. Just because finding food is more challenging doesn't mean I need to change my ways."

"And when there's no food left? Of any kind? When it's below freezing? Kay, you won't last much longer. Not if you don't go to them."

"I don't need them or anybody else. I'll pull through on my own."

And just as they have many times before, these stern words end their discussion. Bill's right, of course. About the food. About everything. But she'll find some other way. Anything but joining the animal-eating outcasts that hide on sight.

Kaarina's hand wanders to her neck and finds a scar she got the last time someone suggested she should eat her animals instead of giving them shelter. Or at least let the others eat them. Because who cares what a loner living in an old abandoned barn eats? The carved line travels from her collar bone, up and across her throat, and onto her cheek.

Standing up for herself—for the animals—may have been considered bravery once upon a time. Stand up against bullying! Defend the weak! These days, for a fit but hopelessly petite twenty-two-year old woman to defy the black market and those who run it is considered nothing less than stupidity. And that stupidity came with a price: a mark on her face to remind her to think twice the next time she considers offering the Unchipped mushrooms and potatoes instead of horse or rabbit meat.

"So you're going to sit there daydreaming until the bears come for you? Come on, Kay. It's just a shoe. How far are we from City of Sweden?"

"Finland. It's City of Finland. How can you still get it wrong? Yes, there was a time when Sweden ruled us."

"I thought it was—"

"Yup, Russia did too. But that was long ago, when things like countries and traveling and politics still existed. Actually, it was even further back than that. When those with schizophrenia were hunted and burned alive for witchcraft. Witches never got to benefit from national healthcare."

"Neither did the United States of America. But you don't see me curled up on a moldy rock, sobbing and moping. Aren't you running out of daylight?"

Irritation jolts her body like an electric shock. Can't he be wrong, just this once? Kaarina gets up and counts to ten. She hopes that this time she'll succeed in holding back the insult lingering on her tongue. It's not that she wants to be a dick to Bill. It's just that there's no one else around these days. Bill gets all of it: the good moods and the bad.

Back on her feet, she hisses to the American man who babbles in her head. "Please find somewhere else to be, would you?? I'm not sobbing or moaning or whining or crying. I needed a breather, is that too much to ask? Quit tapping me, Bill. Go play with one of your toy boys, or make another cheesecake, or whatever it is you do when you're not harassing me."

Her words come out too callous, too strong. Though he's all-knowing and unbelievably annoying, Bill's only trying to help. To keep her going, to get her safely into the city and back. But why does he have to push her buttons—all the wrong ones, all the time?

Shoes sinking into the mucky ground, she listens to her body, her mind. She's alone. Bill's gone, most likely butt-hurt and beyond grumpy. Sulking in his luxury house, high up in the mountains. Slicing avocados and peeling oranges. Sipping a frozen strawberry margarita. Watching the early morning sunbeams hit City of California. *That lucky son of a bitch. He doesn't even know how good he has it.*

"You better keep it together now," she says, unsure whether she's talking to her traitorous shoe or her gloomy and questionable state of mind.

At first she thinks she's just imagining them: careful but determined footsteps behind her, soft on the dead leaves that cover the dirt road leading to City of Finland. Then a bothersome thought creeps up on her. *I'm not alone.*

She stops in her tracks. The leaves rustle for a few seconds longer. Then all falls silent.

Without turning around she takes five steps forward and stops again.

The leaves on the dirt road rustle again. Then the only sound is the steady humming of a nearby utility pole. After all these years, the Chipped still provide power for those living in the suburbs. No matter how many animal carcasses the black market salesmen drag into the city or how many Unchipped spit in the guards' faces. Despite the attacks at the Server-Center. The threats made against the head of the Chip-Center. Despite all these things, the city has never taken action against the rebels, not outside the stone wall.

Some say it shows character on the part of the Chipped. *Kindness.* And some say it's just a matter of time until the Chipped come for them. That the only reason the Unchipped still enjoy their freedom is because the head of the city is occupied with more pressing things, such as creating super computers and un-rubbery vegan bacon. For now—the underdogs wait. They know they'll be dealt with sooner or later.

Kaarina takes off running, leaping over puddles and the occasional tree branch tossed across the road by yesterday's wind. Then she stops.

Rustle. Rustle. Rustle. Her stalker stops and waits. A deep sigh escapes her chapped lips before she turns around.

"Ässä, what are you doing here? I told you, you can't come, not this time." Kaarina stares at the small Jack Russell Terrier that used to belong to her mother. The dog sits in the middle of the road, his head cocked to one side. "I'm telling you, it's not safe."

His head tilts to the other side, tail wagging slowly left, then right, like it's asking a careful question. Asking Kaarina to confirm her decision. A faint whine reaches her ears.

"They'll eat you, buddy. I'm not kidding."

Two sharp barks break the silence between them. Then Ässä turns around and takes off to the woods. Devastated each time one of the animals around her dies, Kaarina knows by now that she shouldn't give them names. She knows, yet around the small barn— the center of her shrunken universe—only a few of the animals haven't been named. The cats that come and go are the only ones who remain nameless, but it's just because Kaarina thinks their anonymity suits their independence. But Kaarina wasn't the one who gave the Jack Russell his name. It had been her mother.

She watches Ässä run back into the woods, disappearing into the thick tree line. The *hum* around her lulls her into a false sense of calm, where nothing bad can happen to those she lives with. Ever. Though the trick Ässä just pulled—the fact that he followed her this far into the open—suggests this is nothing but wishful thinking. She'd prefer it if Ässä was too uncomfortable to come this near the city, with or without her.

A neon-blue light seems to ooze from the city in the distance, both cold and tempting. A two-meter-high stone wall surrounds the city, with two towers marking the main gateway. The wall gives the city the appearance of a bombed-out medieval castle.

Kaarina already knows the guards won't slow her passage. There'll be no ticket or code needed for entry, either. She's not known to be a troublemaker. Why would she be? She'd give away everything to live inside those walls again.

CHAPTER 2
THE CITY

The adrenaline spike hits her just before she reaches the city center. Kaarina stops by a lonely and leafless maple tree, careful not to step on the neon-blue tiles that snake around the hologram platforms and three-story buildings of the downtown area. The solar tiles on the buildings reflect a gentle blue glow, gathering sunlight and powering the city. To see a piece of nature here, like a tree or a rosebush, is rare. To hear a bird sing or a cricket chirp is unheard of.

People wearing bright blue overalls and matching footwear march by. All of them are wearing government-issued, augmented-reality glasses. Some nod at each other, but no one stops to say hello. They're all too rushed or unsure or scared to stop and chat.

She watches them stop and read a brightly lit sign or one of the digital bulletin boards that rise at intervals along the side of the tile road. A young woman passes her, listening to a tune through her wireless earplugs and humming along. A middle-aged man talks on his invisible phone. The phone, the glasses, and the invisible earplugs all use the same system—a microchip implant attached to the cerebral cortex. Back at the Chip-Center people called the system "CS," the Chip-System.

A young girl walks by, about five or six years old. The woman whose hand she's holding looks beefy and stern. The girl's eyes lock on the rip in Kaarina's shoe before going wide with wonder.

"Nursie Laitinen, look! Her shoes. They have holes in them!"

Rooting her little blue sneakers to the ground, the girl pulls on the older woman's hand and tries to make her stop. Pink lips form a letter O. Round blue eyes blink fast, still staring at the mysterious footwear. She's never seen anything so weathered and misshapen in her entire life.

The girl's hand reaches for her AR-glasses to pull them away from her eyes. She wants to steal a quick peek outside the augmented reality, just to better investigate this miraculous gaffe in the system. But Nurse Laitinen tugs her forward.

"Don't stare, Alina, it's not polite."

Rather than defying her nurse's authority, the girl pouts and stomps her sneaker once on the blue tile. Then she continues her journey toward the blue brick building in front of them. As Alina is pulled inside the revolving doors, she looks over her shoulder. Little hand waving cheerfully, she smiles happily at the stranger with such questionable footwear. Kaarina lifts her hand to wave back, but Alina has already disappeared into the softly glowing Children's-Center.

Three short steps take her closer to the tile road, but not too close. She doesn't want to draw any more attention from the pedestrians passing by. None of the billboards or street signs are useful to her: they're all empty of text, symbols, or instructions. Of course, they're not really empty. It's just that she can't see the text they display, unlike like those with AR-glasses. The Chipped live in an augmented reality filled with clear directions, inspiring quotes and adverts, vibrant colors, perfect weather, and stunning outfits.

Or so Kaarina has been told.

For the blue-suited people, the leafless maple tree she leans on is rich with vibrant, healthy leaves. In reality— Kaarina's reality—the only vibrant color to be seen is blue. It glows against the gray buildings, the poles and billboards, and the plants around. It burns her eyes while she walks on the colorless pavement beside the neon-blue tiles.

Stepping on the tiles is not a good idea. If she did, the bright-blue blur would attack her like a lightning strike. Then a raging headache would kick in. She'd soon feel nauseated and unbalanced. She doesn't know what it is that makes her sick if she tries to walk on the tiles–whether it's the flawed microchip in her brain, or simply the lack of AR-glasses. There's no one around to ask, no one to compare notes with.

She steps over the small cracks in the pavement like a child, heading toward the east side of the city. This is where she can still find small stores and apartment complexes. Where things still look a bit like they did before the city was redesigned around augmented reality. This is not too far from where Kaarina's mother used to live.

The Pedalers—people who pedal electric bikes to earn their keep—live on the east side. Not in poor conditions but not wealthy, either.

Only a few people work at the stores and pharmacies. Food, clothing, and medicine are all provided to the Chipped by the government. Nobody knows for sure why these stores are still open, but some say it's only because some people refused to leave their old jobs. The Chipped use their chip-credits, or CCs, for other things: AR-clothing and accessories, virtual pets, fashionable digital haircuts, and bronze-but-natural-looking tans. The better they look in other people's eyes, the better they must feel about themselves.

The CS lets them rank other people from one to five stars after every interaction. Social rank is stored in the database, along with name, address, age, family history, medical records, and possible issues in the chipping process or in adjusting to the augmented reality.

Kaarina is in the system just like everyone else. She's categorized as *Unchipped, location unknown.*

There was a time, right after her unsuccessful chip

installation, when she worried that they'd come after her, drag her back into the Chip-Center for testing and probing and slicing. She was afraid the utility poles would be turned off: a sign of war between the Chipped and Unchipped.

But they never came for her.

Finding her wouldn't have cost them too much effort. Unwilling to relocate too far from her apartment, she had chosen a hiding place near enough to walk into the city, but far enough from the suburbs where the rest of the Unchipped lived. She wasn't the only one who didn't want to live in the Chip-Center as the city's newest science project.

Most of the old apartments and houses were unsafe to live in, either because of the risk of collapse or the restlessness of the neighborhood's new inhabitants. The Unchipped who ran the black market were unpredictable and murderous, though they mostly focused on hunting down the animals that roamed in the woods. As a fierce animal lover, Kaarina refused to join them. She hid in the barn where she used to work, mucking stalls and taking care of a dozen horses. Her horse friends were still around, but they were no longer locked in the stalls or paddocks. They had quickly learned to avoid people. If anyone other than Kaarina approached the barn they would turn and run.

Days, weeks, months, and finally years passed by, and Kaarina was left alone at the barn where she chose to live among the animals. No visits from either the

Chip-Center employees or the guards in charge of public safety.

After a full year of living in the woods, lurking near the city line but never entering, Kaarina had finally pushed her luck. She paid a visit to the city inside the stone walls. Walked around. Touched things: buildings, poles and hologram stands, even people. She purposely bumped into the blue suits, hoping they wouldn't report her to the guards for invading their personal space. After all, touch wasn't something people dealt with very well these days.

Nothing happened.

She stood near a city employee, out in the open. She walked by a guard close to the Chip-Center.

Nothing.

Air—that's all she was to them. It was like their AR-glasses couldn't even spot her. Except that small gestures kept giving them away: a quick side-eye or a nervous glance, followed by hurried footsteps in the opposite direction. They were eager to put as much distance as possible between themselves and the creature that couldn't be ranked—a thing that didn't fit into their reality.

Kaarina no longer worries about being caught. The paved path leads up a small hill as she enters the east side of the city. Here the trees and plants still demand their space, covering the sides of the buildings and the small horseshoe-shaped park. The blue-tile-snake still wiggles across and around the area, but fewer glowing bulletin boards and screens decorate the streets. The apartment complexes take up most of the open area. Down here at street level, blank signs glow brightly in front of the stores. If Kaarina remembers right, the pharmacy sign is the one in the middle: slightly crooked, possibly off its hinge, but not enough for the owner to straighten it.

She sits down on a park bench, carefully scanning the area. One person—that's all she needs. One blue suit to barter with. Then she'll have to leave this place and disappear into the darkening woods, just like she has a handful of times before.

There aren't many blue suits around to choose from. Kaarina bends her legs to hide her broken sneakers underneath the bench. As if it would matter. She could sit here shoeless, pantsless, topless. Or she could wear the highest quality, most expensive winter gear from the ruins of some sporting goods store. Whatever she wore, people would circle around to avoid her as if she carried the plague.

A woman approaches from the distance, her arm held down at her side as if she's holding a leash. Fingers wrapped around something invisible, her plump blue figure sways slowly by.

"Cute dog," Kaarina says, trying her luck. The woman turns her head in surprise. She focuses her AR-glasses to see who has complimented her virtual pet. When the visor turns to scan the park bench, Kaarina nods toward the spot where she thinks the digital Fifi stands. Or sits. Or barks. It might as well be attacking her leg, ripping open her skin and flesh while her blood spatters on the pavement between her and the staring dogwalker. She'll never know.

The woman chuckles nervously. She's probably wearing screaming-red lipstick, to go with a hot and trendy boiler suit or a puff shoulder top, accompanied by a nautical color wrap dress—whatever the latest virtual fashion trend is. Kaarina doesn't know. She doesn't really care. But she does need the woman's help.

"Would you have a minute or two to help me out? I'm here to—"

The dogwalker turns and walks away on her imaginary block heels, discarding Kaarina's entire existence.

"What a bitch. I could see that coming a mile away."

"Shut it, Bill. You're not helping."

"I will, as soon as you start making smarter choices. Pick one that seems under the weather. Work smarter, not harder."

Kaarina doesn't respond. Instead, she looks around, scanning the quiet area for her next target.

Old man crossing the street.

A kid running backwards, catching an invisible ball with a baseball glove. Or so Kaarina thinks. She can only see the glove.

Another digital-dog walker, carefully picking up imaginary droppings into a virtual poop bag, then ditching it in a trash can by the road.

"Fake dog owners are the worst. Do you know what those puppies cost in the virtual market? You could buy a small house with that kind of credit."

"At least they want to take care of someone, not just themselves. Could be a sign of a need to nurture."

"I think you're one fry short of a happy meal."

A new blue suit approaches and interrupts Kaarina's fiery retort. Her hungry eyes stare at the potential prey. The guy is about her age, maybe a few years older, fitter than most blue suits she's seen in the city.

Greasy vegan food isn't a problem when you can buy curves or a leaner form on the virtual store and look exactly like you want to look. With the nightly order-in service the city offers its tenants, most people can't resist the temptation to order something tasty but less than healthy. Or at least that's what Kaarina witnessed during her brief stay at the Chip-Center. There are only two things the city offers equally to all tenants, Chipped and Unchipped: food and pills.

As the fit blue suit walks closer, Kaarina notices another interesting detail about him: he's in desperate need of a haircut. Those who live in the augmented reality rarely keep their real hair long. Short or shaved hair is much more convenient to bathe with.

"That's it, that's your guy. Go get it, girl."

Resisting the urge to remind Bill that he's not a twenty-year-old cheerleader, Kaarina stands up and takes the few strides that separate her from the tile road. Hands shoved deep into her hoodie pockets, she lifts her chin and smiles. The guy slows at her gesture, but he hasn't stopped yet. Kaarina waves her hand halfheartedly.

"Hey man, you in a rush? Could I borrow a few

seconds of your time?"

He stops, looks right at her through the tinted visor. "You are…" he begins but is too hesitant to continue.

"I'm what?"

"You know…"

Kaarina takes a deep breath before she replies. "You mean one of *those* people? Well, yes I am. That's me. One hundred percent. But I don't bite or have the plague or anything. This state of my so-called life is not contagious. I could just use a helping hand, is all."

He stands still, his pose mirroring hers: hands deep in his pockets, feet shoulder-width apart. They stand and peer at each other. She can almost hear his chipped brain ticking: contemplating whether he should keep on going or stay and hear her out. Finally, he reaches for his AR-glasses, pulls them off his head.

"I was going to ask if you were lost or something. I obviously know what… *who* you are."

"Oh, we've met before?"

"No, we haven't, I mean that you… you're obviously not Chipped."

"Oh, that. What gave me away? The lack of AR-glasses? Or the fact that I look like a hungry hobo?"

Making fun of him is a terrible idea, she knows. But being treated like a parasite each time she's among the Chipped is finally starting to push her over the edge. The Unchipped aren't any better—they want her to produce meat for the black market, after all—but at least they talk to her like she's a real person, not some braindead excuse for a human being.

"I didn't... I don't think you look like a hobo. I think you're quite beautiful, actually." His hand flies up to cover his mouth, like he's trying to push his unexpected words back into the hole they slipped out of.

"You what?"

"You're really pretty. Even that... your scar," he nods toward her face. "I think it makes you unique, more human somehow."

Kaarina investigates his face, trying to find a trace of sarcasm or mockery. But the only thing she finds is sincerity and shyness. If this guy won't help her, no one will. If it wasn't a matter of life and death, she'd scold herself for being so calculative. Though his being kind doesn't automatically mean that he'll help her out. She needs to startle him somehow. Truly get his attention.

"You want to touch it?"

He blinks rapidly and huffs. "Um... what?"

"My scar."

He shifts his weight from one foot to another. "I don't... I, umm..."

Kaarina takes a step closer. Her heart beats faster and her face flushes. "Go on. It doesn't hurt or anything. If that's what you're afraid of."

She knows that's not what he's afraid of. He's merely shocked, trying to shake off the discomfort of her unusual suggestion.

"Are you serious?"

"Sure. Unless, you *don't* want to touch it?"

"No, no, no. I mean yes, yes I do, but—"

Kaarina reaches for his hand and runs his fingertips along the scar. The man sucks his lower lip in and stares in wonder. For a moment, he seems like a teenage boy, touching a girl for the first time. The intimacy of the moment and the seriousness of his face almost make Kaarina forget about the task at hand. But only for a fleeting moment.

She lets go of his hand and shrugs. "You afraid you have the pox or something now?"

He scoffs in disbelief. "No… It's just…" His hand is still frozen in midair. "I can't remember the last time someone held my hand. Or the last time I touched someone's face."

Blue eyes meet hers, and they stand quietly, processing their short but strange conversation.

"Well done, Kay. This bonehead is a done deal. Move in for the kill."

Shaking her head to get rid of the man who lives there, Kaarina breaks their stare to close her eyes. *I got this, Bill.* Rubbing her temples compulsively, she must seem like the biggest town crazy this stranger has ever met.

What had they been talking about? Before she let a total stranger touch her?

"Oh, and I guess I should say… thank you? And you too. I mean, you're not pretty, but handsome or, or good-looking…" Kaarina chuckles nervously and spreads her hands in defeat.

And here I thought this couldn't get more awkward than it already was.

"Drugs, Kay. Get the pills. Quit this mumbo-jumbo and focus."

They've both taken a step out of their comfort zones, but the man shows no signs of wanting to leave. They both blush bright pink. Kaarina wets her lips and says, "I'm Kaarina, by the way. People call me Kay."

"I'm people *now in this idiotic game of yours?"*

Shut up, Bill.

"Nice to meet you, Kay. My name is Markus. I'm not really good at this, so please forgive me. Or I guess I'm just a bit rusty. I don't really talk to strangers that often."

She should ask him about helping her. Now, before the moment's gone. But she's too intrigued not to ask, "Who do you talk to, then?"

"Huh?"

"If you don't talk to strangers, who do you talk to?"

Considering her question, Markus looks up to the sky, then gives a small laugh.

"I guess I don't really talk to anyone these days."

"Not even at work?"

"At work, yes, I used to. But not after I got promoted from pedaling and moved to the Server-Center. I'm out cold most of my workday, so when you think about it, me not talking to a bunch of people kind of makes sense."

She's heard of the Servers, people who let the city

plug them into the CS. They lend their brains for use as computer servers to help run the city's augmented reality. It's been a wild rumor among the Unchipped, but Kaarina had never heard it confirmed—until now.

Markus brings his thumb up to his mouth, bites the nail a few times like he's contemplating whether to say something or not. "And what about you?"

"What about me?"

"You don't live in the city."

"Oh, I don't?" She realizes her sarcasm is lost on him. "No, I don't live here. Which brings me to—"

"What's that like?" Markus asks, sounding a bit out of breath. "I've heard that the Unchipped get all the best food. What did you have for breakfast this morning? What do you do all day and night?"

Kaarina dodges his piercing but friendly gaze. She shrugs and says, "I eat what I can find. Mushrooms and dry bread, mostly. Not exactly culinary treats if you ask me."

"And where do you work?"

It's a fair question, but it still makes Kaarina laugh. "Staying alive is a full time job." She bites her lip so she won't tell Markus about the bloodthirsty Unchipped that lurk around the woods. After all, in Markus's eyes, isn't Kaarina one of them? She can't scare him away. Not when she's this close to getting what she needs. "I take care of sick animals, horses mostly. The barn I live in has cats and rabbits and dogs as well. I make sure nobody goes hungry, though at this point, they've pretty much figured the lay of the land."

Markus's wide eyes drill into Kaarina. "What else? Do you swim? Climb trees? Do you visit the old amusement park?"

Is this how the Chipped envision her life? Sports and Ferris wheels?

"I have a few paperbacks I like to read. But at this point, I already remember every word by heart."

He stares at her in awe for such a long time that Kaarina thinks he's returned into the augmented reality and started binge-watching some movie about scavengers that ride roller-coasters and fine-dine in fancy restaurants.

After what seems like a long time, Markus snaps out of his trance.

"That must be something else, having so much freedom. And your barn sounds like a great place to live." He stops gnawing on his thumbnail. "Anyway, I should get going," he says. He gives her an awkward bow and turns to leave.

"No, wait!"

Without thinking, she steps onto the blue tiles to block his way, then doubles over at the surge of pain in her head. Markus grabs her arms and gently walks her backwards, until she sits firmly on the park bench again. The AR-glasses lie abandoned on the tile road, with a sizable crack across the visor. He has dropped them when hurrying to help Kaarina.

"Are you okay? Wow, I had no idea that's what... that's how..."

43

Unsure how to finish his sentence, Markus sits down next to her. He twists his hands awkwardly, then crosses them over his chest.

"I'm okay, it's all right. Those sons of bitches just zap me like a motherfucker."

His eyes widen in shock. Is it because of the curse words or the fact that she's uttered them? When he bursts out laughing, Kaarina half expects him to fall off the bench. The power of his laughter shakes his body. She can't keep her lips from twitching too, and soon she's laughing along with him, lulled into a strange emotion she'd forgotten a long time ago.

"Man, you both crazy. I'm outta here."

Bill leaving reminds Kaarina of the task at hand. She turns to Markus, who is still trying to collect himself.

"Listen, I do need your help with something. I have a… friend, who's fighting an infection. He desperately needs antibiotics. You can probably guess that I don't have any CC's. But I do have something you may be interested in."

From her hoodie pocket, she pulls out a small, furry object: a brown rabbit's foot.

Soon after The Great Affliction, people stopped believing in God and saints, Heaven and Hell. Suddenly religion was no longer a thing. The CS has taken over. People also started to find comfort in ideas like good and bad karma, or objects like crystals, healing minerals, and lucky charms. There are only two things the Unchipped can use to barter with the Chipped:

talismans like this rabbit's foot, and animal meat.

"A rabbit foot? Wow, I haven't seen one of these since I was in kindergarten…" Markus takes the foot from her, turns it around in his hands, then hands it back to her. "But I'm afraid I don't believe in magic or luck or higher powers. You should keep your foot, save it for a rainy day."

"You're not going to help me then?"

"For a hairy piece of good luck? No, that's not what I want from you."

Eyes still locked on Markus, Kaarina shoves the rabbit foot back into her pocket.

Alarms and red flags, that's what she should be seeing right now, but for some reason her gut isn't sending her any warning signals. Maybe she should tap Bill, ask him for advice. But she already knows what her telepathic companion would say. He'd call Markus a potential psycho, a possible rapist, or alternatively, a serial killer.

He could be right, of course. It's not unheard of. Though people do feel better, thanks to the chipping, the daily antidepressants, and the Happiness-Program, there are still plenty of mentally unstable individuals out there, blending in with the rest.

Kaarina holds her gaze steady. Without the medicine, Rocky is as good as dead. The infection is already making it hard for him to breathe. With a slight shake of the head, she says, "The rabbit foot is all I have to give. Nothing else you see is for sale."

His smile is shy, nothing like a sociopath's smile. Although, how would she know? She's the crazy person here, not him. She's the stranger in a strange land.

Markus gets up from the bench and breaks the silence. "Tell you what. How much do you need?"

Relieved to focus on a math problem instead of wondering whether she's about to get raped, sliced and gutted, Kaarina counts with her fingers. Math's never been something she excels in. Triple-checking and counting the amount seems like a good idea.

"I need two hundred pills. And it must be doxycycline."

"Wow! What does this animal have? Sepsis?" When Kaarina doesn't reply, Markus continues his rant. "And to need that amount of antibiotics, he must weigh, what? Two hundred kilos?"

"Closer to seven hundred. Are you going to help me or what?"

Rubbing the bridge of his nose, Markus silently sits back on the bench. His chin lifted, he gazes up at the sky. Maybe he expects the answer to this puzzle to fall through the dull blanket of clouds, straight into his lap.

"Didn't this moron just say that he wasn't superstitious?"

Blue suits pass by them on the tile road. They peek curiously at the strange couple, sitting next to each other on a park bench. Then they eyeball Markus's abandoned AR-glasses, forgotten in the middle of the tile road. Curious but too scared to stop or ask, they continue their walk along the blue tiles. They'll never learn what the Unchipped and the Chipped could possibly have in common.

Oblivious to their stares, Markus has clearly forgotten his reality—the reality he's taking an unexpected break from. Eyes investigating the sky, he seems to be lost in some sort of inner turmoil. Finally, he nods and locks eyes with Kaarina, gives her yet another careful smile.

"Two hundred pills it is then. You said doxycycline?"

Head snapping back in surprise, she does her best to recover from this sudden development. And she needs to do it fast. She has taken all the time she can afford as her companion back home fights for his life. "Can you afford it? Do you have enough CC's?"

"Yes, I've got plenty. And medicine doesn't cost that much these days. Most people just order what they need with their dinner and nightly pills. It's all covered by the government."

Tempted to ask more about the pills she never took, the ones that everyone here swallows on daily basis, Kaarina forces herself to stay focused on her task. Markus gets up from the bench and wipes his hands on the back of his overalls. Smile deepening, he raises his eyebrows. Kaarina has forgotten to answer his previous question.

"Yes, doxycycline. And that's wild, medicine being so cheap. Do you think they'll have enough? I mean, because people hardly need to buy stuff from the pharmacy?"

Markus walks back to the tile road, picks up his AR-glasses. "One way to find out." He turns his back on her and starts toward the crooked sign.

"Wait!"

At her call, Markus slows his stride and turns around. He continues his walk backwards, eyebrows raised in a question. Kaarina speeds toward the road but stops before reaching the tiles. The road is too wide for her to jump over. She hollers instead.

"I thought you didn't want the rabbit foot!"

Markus grins happily, keeps walking backwards, and shouts back. "You're right, I don't want it! But you already paid me!"

He turns around, only a few feet away from the pharmacy. Kaarina looks left and right, backs up to get some momentum, and leaps over the tiles, touching the surface only twice until she's on the other side. Squeezing the rabbit foot in her fist, she catches up with Markus, reaching for his shoulder. He stops and turns around to face her.

"What do you mean I already paid you? Am I in debt to you somehow?"

"You don't owe me a thing."

"What then? I don't get it."

Markus loops the AR-glasses around his neck but doesn't put them back on. Avoiding Kaarina's questioning eyes, he smiles and shrugs once.

"It's been months, no, *years* since I've had a conversation with someone without having to watch my every word. A low social rank is no joke, it could cost me my job. I'm good right now but need to make sure it stays that way. This makes me extra careful when I talk with anybody. If I talk with anybody, that is. I'm this close," he holds his thumb and forefinger a few inches apart, "to leaving my apartment and getting a house of my own. They don't grant houses to single people, not usually. But I'm not going to push my luck and ask them why they made an exception with me. To get my house I need to score high. Below-average rank would be a deal breaker."

"Okay…" Kaarina says, her brow furrowed, "but I still don't get why you're helping me or how I've paid you. Just because we chatted on the bench and I let you touch my face?"

"Yup. That's it."

"For a two-minute chat, you'll buy me a shit-ton of meds?"

"I'm telling you, I can't remember the last time I laughed as hard as I just did. In fact, I can't remember the last time I laughed at all. You make me… you make me feel good. Better than I remember feeling in years."

Stunned, her mouth partly open, Kaarina shifts her weight from one foot to another. Then it hits her, the opportunity. Out of the blue, lucky as can be. Has her rabbit foot finally started to pull its weight?

"If you want to do this again, we can. Meet me here again next week? Same place, same time? There are a few other things I could really use…" Her calculated words make her gag. Taking advantage of kind people is not something she'd normally do. But the thought of new, unshredded winter shoes flashes through her mind— distracting, tempting.

Should I take it back? It's a scam. I'm a scam. What if next week he doesn't find me funny at all? But Bill is not there to answer her questions.

Markus's smile deepens. A single nod seals their deal. He puts on the AR-glasses and reaches for the pharmacy's door handle.

"It's a date."

Kaarina walks through the dark woods, holding a paper bag filled with pill boxes. Her excellent night vision is not enough to guide her back home, so she's turned on her headlamp. Praying the batteries don't run out, she estimates that she's only twenty minutes away from the barnyard.

Rocky will be there waiting. The other animals might be there too: they usually check in around supper time.

Humming a tune that could be from her past, or could be one that she just made up, she gets closer to the suburbs and further away from the city, from the zapping blue tiles—from Markus. It's impossible to shake the image of his overgrown hair and amused blue eyes. A wide grin takes over Kaarina's usually serious face. Rolling her eyes, she tells herself that her cheerful mood is just because she has just scored a bagful of free antibiotics. That's all there is to it.

A wolf howls in the distance. Her steps hurried, she moves faster and deeper into the woods. She picks up a steady jog, already dreaming of her nightly supper. She can almost taste the green tea and rye crackers.

The groceries will have to wait. Tomorrow she'll make another trip. The shop deeper in the village and by the brook hasn't been cleaned out yet, or at least she's never heard or sensed anyone walking down there.

What will happen after she's cleaned out this last source of nutrition? In the dead of winter, alone in the woods? Will she start farming? In one of the abandoned greenhouses by the suburbs? Endless images of dead and dying houseplants flash through her mind. Nope, farming's not an option. Starving to death might be.

The distribution center run by the Unchipped community is not an option either. The group of fifty or sixty outcasts have taken over the center, controlling who gets what and for what price.

For Kaarina to do business with them, she'd need to bring animal meat. She would have to kill one of her companions. The Unchipped know she protects the animals. Luckily the animals around the barn are smart enough to flee the scene whenever a stranger approaches. It's like they know what the outcasts are there for.

Until now, Kaarina's been able to find some canned and dry goods, nuts, seeds, dry beans, and crisp breads from smaller shops located further away from the

Unchipped community. The selection was poor from the get-go, but now it's starting to wither away to nothing.

Another howl echoes through the forest, interrupting her hungry thoughts. Her jog turns into a full run. Because of her soaking wet socks, her freezing feet have started to send cool shivers through her body. It'll take hours to get warm. She'll need to turn on the small space heater tonight, get snug inside a doubled-up sleeping bag.

Then something else reaches her ears. The sound echoes through the woods, stops her in her tracks. Out of breath, shivering with cold, she freezes to listen. Has she imagined it?

There it is again. A horse—whinnying in distress. She can't see the barnyard but she already knows who it is. There's no other option. Any other horse would run away from a stressful situation. Rocky wouldn't, he can't. He's too weak.

She takes off running. What has upset Rocky badly enough for him to cry for help like this? Has the barn roof collapsed? A wolf wandered too close? Usually they stay away, focusing on deer or badgers or raccoon dogs.

Her ripped shoe gets stuck in the mud, slips off, and lands on the path. Not stopping to pick it up, Kaarina sprints toward the dimly lit barnyard. Against her usual habit, she's left the light on so Rocky can rest in one of the bedded stalls downstairs.

A dozen shadows dance wildly under the dim outdoor light. The barn doors are wide open, the other sliding door hanging off its hinges. Rocky rears on his hind legs, kicks with his front. All around him people dodge his hooves–some holding knives, some syringes.

"Hey! HEY!"

The Unchipped stop their dance and turn toward Kaarina's fierce voice. Twenty strides and she's at the barnyard. Barging through the crowd, she races straight to Rocky and places herself between the foaming horse and their uninvited guests.

There are ten of them, maybe more standing guard in the shadows. Restrained hostility lingering on every face, they loom still and stare at Kaarina and the horse. Heart pounding out of her chest, she searches the crowd for a leader. A man three times her size steps forward.

"Good evening, Kid. You're home late this evening." He cocks his head, eyes narrowed and fixed on hers. A low grunt reaches Kaarina's ears. A new Unchipped leader, one that Kaarina hasn't met before. He seems too young to lead a wild crowd like that. Kaarina estimates he's in his late twenties.

His face is marked by several cuts and bruises. His wide frame rises in front of her, sturdy and indestructible as a mountain. Like the leader before him, the man looks confident, strong—and wary. But there is something different about him. Something about his face. His eyes.

Sadness.

Kaarina forces herself to stand her ground, refuses to take a step back. Rocky snorts behind her, his muzzle poking the pharmacy bag Kaarina's holding.

"Why the hell didn't you stash those pills, Kay? Hide them, quick. This Yeti is not here to play house or exchange greetings."

Careful not to speak to Bill out loud, Kaarina answers him inside her head. *What do I do, Bill? What the hell do I do?*

"Just relax, he's here for the horse, not you."

For the love of god, Bill!

"Okay, okay. Just answer him. Talk your way out of this. You just scored a bagful of meds for a five-minute talk with a guy you've never met. Not even a private escort gets paid that well."

Her mouth opens but no words come out. She's too terrified to talk. The memory of the Unchipped leader's knife digging into her face flashes through her mind. With a slightly amused look on his face, the Yeti cocks his head, waiting. She presses her lips together, opens her mouth to try again. Nothing.

"Jesus on a bike, Kay! You look like a blow-up doll."

"Not in a chatty mood, then." The Yeti's low voice rumbles. "Well, we're heading back to the center after our little shopping trip. It seems like we've completely missed all food supply at your neck of woods. The store by the brook had some good stuff left on its shelves."

The Yeti nods at a slim, mean-looking Unchipped man carrying a black trash bag: the rest of Kaarina's food supply. All of it. Gone. Like an objection to her oncoming starvation, her stomach grumbles loudly.

"Imagine our surprise when we saw a light on at the barn here. I suggested we take a look. And what do we find? Seven hundred kilos of meat, that's what. It must be my lucky day."

Kaarina takes a step back and presses her back against Rocky. The man's dark eyes drill into Kaarina's, then wander further down…

"But look, what do we have here…" He slowly steps closer, until he's so close that Kaarina can smell smoke and firewood and animal blood on him.

She can't breathe. Can't move. She closes her eyes, hoping that what's to come will be over soon.

Rocky snorts again, his front hoof pawing at the gravel.

"Say, Kid. Would you like to trade that gelding for a pair of winter boots?"

"Kick this asshole, Kay. Break his teeth."

You want me dead? He'll knock me out if I do.

"Or maybe there's something else I could take instead of your wild stallion…" Kaarina hears the mountain of a man move closer. Dark shades and dim light spin across her closed eyelids. She's held her breath for too long. But she's too scared to move away from the Yeti.

Just as she opens her eyes, she feels his rough hand on hers. Slowly yet demanding, one finger at a time, the man loosens Kaarina's grip on the paper bag. The scar on her cheek throbs, the pain of her past stopping Kaarina from fighting for what's rightfully hers. Instead, she simply watches as her treasure is stolen right out of her hand.

The Yeti turns and rummages through the pharmacy bag with his back to her. Eyes wild, she shakes her head in despair. Without the antibiotics she may as well hand Rocky over to be sold on the black market. With no food left, she might as well take a knee and beg the Yeti to take her with him and bring her to the suburbs. Just the thought of living with these animal-killing predators makes her gag.

She takes a sudden step toward the Yeti and his peers.

"Stop right there, Kay-Kay. Don't be stupid."

She catches herself right before she answers Bill out loud. *You know how badly I need those antibiotics, Bill.*

"What I know is that we need you alive. What good will the drugs do, without you here to feed them to that damn horse? I'm telling you, step away from the Yeti. Now."

She does as she's told. The Unchipped leader, so close to her still, turns his eyes to her. Kaarina feels her face burn with confusion and anger. Being at his mercy, so weak and powerless… it stings more than her likely fate of soon starving to death. Head spinning, she wonders if it'll leave a permanent mark on her, some sort of a brand. Though she knows she's delusional, the thought of being marked as the Unchipped's property makes her feel vulnerable and small. How is she supposed to fight a dozen of them? Alone, and without a weapon?

The Yeti hands the paper bag to a woman standing nearby. Her shaved head is like an egg, her eyes cold and hard like glass.

"Wonder if this lunatic ever blinks."

Glass-Eye folds the paper bag into a bundle and tucks it under her arm. A small, mocking smile lingers on her face. Her jaw moves slowly from side to side as she stares Kaarina down.

"You know what, forget about Yeti. I would keep my eyes on this conniving witch instead."

You're not helping, Bill.

"It's been a pleasure doing business with you, Kid. We'll do you a kindness and leave your horse be," a hand in a fingerless glove salutes Rocky, "as he's obviously not currently suitable for consumption. But not to worry, Kid. You've proved your worth. Obviously you're quite useful in many other ways."

His deep gaze makes her stomach turn. For a terrifying second she's sure she'll vomit on the Yeti's shoes. The double meaning of his words is not lost on Kaarina. Or is it just her fear, reading nonexistent meanings between the lines? She clears her throat but the words fail her again.

"Okay guys, time to roll. Our friend here must be tired after her shoe-dropping adventures in the woods. No need to be rude and overstay our welcome."

With a low murmur, the Unchipped turn and start back toward the dark woods. The Yeti stands still, sizing her up. Kaarina gasps for air but meets his gaze. A

57

crooked grin deepens on his scarred face.

"You're practically mute, but you act like you got a pair. I can respect that."

When she's sure she's about to pass out from all the spinning, Kaarina closes her eyes.

A pair of combat boots thump against the ground. He's finally leaving, following his crowd into the woods.

"Until we meet again, Kid."

CHAPTER 3
2 YEARS EARLIER

"What. The actual. Fuck. Is going on?"

The voice is inside her head but it's not her own. In her foggy state of mind, she wonders if the hospital has an AI, like the one her mother's house used to have. What was it called? Mirva? Miranda?

"Who names an AI Miranda?"

Puzzled and dizzy, she tries to ignore the man talking inside her head.

The half-circle room is crowded with beds, each separated from the others by a white hospital curtain. An assortment of surgical instruments covers the wheeled metal cart next to Kaarina's bed. One of the tools points at her like a weapon. It looks a lot like a drill. A stain of blood decorates her hospital gown.

A deafening, monotonous beeping is the only sound she hears. The nurse rushed out twenty-four minutes and thirty seconds ago. She keeps staring at the clock above the entrance. All she can do is count the minutes and seconds as they go by. Everything else is too foggy and unfocused.

They're all asleep, everyone but her. In the middle of the beeping. White hospital socks poke out from the bottom of every bed. The hospital curtains don't reach that far. Privacy is not a high priority here. After all, nobody in this room should be awake.

"Hey, homie? Care to check in? What is this place?"

The voice startles her. She loses count of the minutes. Sitting up in the bed, she waits for the nurse to come back. Or for someone—anyone—to come and unplug her from the heavy brain scanner still attached to her head. She could have done that much, the nurse. She could have unplugged Kaarina from this uncomfortable device before she took off, gasping "We have another one" into her invisible walkie-talkie.

"Okay, could you please explain what's happening? Who the fuck are you? Why am I seeing you? Do you even speak English?"

"Finnish… I speak Finnish," she whispers.

"Ha! It talks! And in fluent English too. Thanks for joining this madness."

"Why are you here?"

The man huffs, momentarily lost for words. *"That's the thing, girl. I'm not there. See, last I checked, I was in the City of California Medical-Center, getting my chip treatment. All was swell. And then I wake up. I'm still here, but not really, because I'm staring at your pale white-girl face. This is not the AR-shit I was promised. Or is it? Is this part of the treatment?*

Some sick way to test our mental health?"

She listens to the voice, turning her focus inward, to herself. As she closes her eyes, images of a room—another hospital—flash on her closed eyelids. Hands and arms gesture wildly. A man, at least ten years older than her, his skin many shades darker than her own. She looks out past the broad window she's never seen before to the skyscrapers rising on every side, sunbeams piercing the air between them. This is a place she's never been before. Not that she's there now either. Not really.

"Where are you? *Who* are you?"

"The name's William. The place I already told you. I'm in City of California."

"You're from the United States?"

"No such thing left, hon. You should know this. Only West-Land remains. And the cities. Sounds like you're from East-Land yourself. Sweden? Why are there dark shades in front of the windows there? Let me see outside."

"Finland. And you can't. It's already dark."

"Oh, so it's four a.m. there, not p.m.?"

Her eyes go back to the clock on the wall, the same one William must be staring at—through her eyes or mind or being or some higher existence. Her head turns until she finds what she's looking for. A digital clock by the lab table tells her the exact time of day. Sixteen hundred, sharp.

"No, it's still daytime."

"It's already dark at four o'clock in the afternoon? Girl, what kind of a special hell do you live in?"

Her head spins with weird sensations and exhaustion. She counts the minutes again.

Forty-two. Forty-three. Forty-four.

The strange man in her head won't stop talking. He blabbers along, flustered and bewildered, talking through emotions that Kaarina surely should be feeling as well.

"...so maybe this is a chipping phase, and just a part of—"

"I don't think this was supposed to happen," Kaarina says, interrupting him. "I think something has gone terribly wrong."

When William doesn't respond to her, she continues. "I think the chip didn't take. And they messed up something in our brain."

"What does that have to do with you and me?"

"I don't know," she huffs. "It must have... connected us to each other somehow."

"Like telepathic allies and shit? That's insane!"

Kaarina nods. She sees William burying his face into his hands. "It is insane. But I also know you're flustered and rubbing your face in despair. How could I know this, if this wasn't because of the chip? If not for the chip, then how are we even having this conversation?"

Bill spreads his hands. *"You're right,"* he says. *"You are so fucking right. This is insane. We're insane. What the hell are we going to do?"*

"That's what we need to figure out, I guess. And I think we should do it together."

The door opens. Two nurses in blue overalls walk in. A doctor wearing a white lab-coat follows. Kaarina giggles at the scene, though she's not sure why. Something about the nurses' expressions make them look like cartoon characters. Looney Tunes, ready for action.

The doctor seems calm, almost serene. "Look who's awake. How are you, Kaarina?" Her voice is soft as silk, pleasant as slowly flowing water.

Kaarina meets her smile and shrugs. "You tell me, doctor." She's glad they're speaking in her native Finnish. For years now, English has been the official language of both East-Land and West-Land. She feels too confused—too off—to dig into her normally fluent English vocabulary.

"Can you please tell this whitecoat to speak English? Because heaven forbid I get to know what the hell is going on."

"Well, my name is Dr. Laura Solomon. I have good news and bad news. Which one…" The doctor's words trail off when Kaarina shakes her head. After giving her an empathic smile, the doctor puts on a pair of AR-glasses and starts tapping into some sort of a digital database Kaarina can't see.

"You're probably wondering why we use such old technology." The doctor's index finger briefly points at the AR-glasses she's wearing. "It's just so much easier to differentiate the realities from one another. For the human mind, it's easier to stay in control of your own mind when you can shut down one reality with a simple hand movement."

"With all due respect, Doctor, *that* is not something I'm wondering about right now."

"Very well then. The procedure went as expected. We were able to install the microchip implant into your cerebral cortex. That is the good news—nothing went wrong. No bleeding or infections, no blood clots or nerve damage. No trace of CSF leaks, all mental functions are working as they should."

"And the bad news?"

The doctor taps on her invisible gadget a few more times until her hand swipes to her left. She takes off the AR-glasses and hands them over to one of the nurses. The other nurse hovers by, unsure where to look and what to do with her hands.

"You're not the first one. You're not alone in this. So please, Kaarina, do not worry, I'm one hundred percent positive we're about to figure out why some of our patients experience this state."

"What state is that? What's wrong with me?"

The doctor moves the metal desk aside and sits at the foot of her bed. Machines beep around them, muffling the whooshing sound in Kaarina's head. Kaarina grabs ahold of the brain scanner, tries to pull it off. The two wide-eyed nurses immediately rush over to stop her.

The doctor gestures at the nurses to leave Kaarina be. "It's okay, it's okay." Gently reaching for the scanner, she pulls something on the side. The whooshing sound disappears with a release of pressure. Doctor Solomon pulls off the scanner and places it on a small empty nightstand by the hospital bed.

"There, that's better. Like I said, the chip is in there, we've got that going for us. It's just that we aren't able to connect you with the Chip-System, the CS. But I can assure you, whatever the error is, we have our best research and IT people looking into it. It could be a matter of days, or even hours, until we figure out the miscalculation and get you plugged into the augmented reality. Then you'll get to be a part of the Happiness-Program. Just as planned."

"There are others like me?" Kaarina rubs the side of her temples, feeling lightheaded but surprisingly normal. "How long have they been unplugged? Where are they now?"

"We estimate that about one in a hundred become Unchipped during the procedure. Most of them are relocated from this hospital to the Chip-Center."

"Most of them? How about the rest of them?"

The nurses exchange a nervous look but the doctor's smile deepens. She reaches for Kaarina's hand, squeezes it tight.

"Only a small fraction of the Unchipped live outside the city. Those who stay with us enjoy housing, food and medicine, an opportunity to work... Kaarina, they have a full life here. They lack for nothing. Just like everyone else, your kind get access to all happiness-pills, as well as the wellness channels."

"Oh no she didn't. Our kind?"

"Even without the chip?"

"That's right. The only difference is that the augmented reality won't work for you outside the Chip-Center. For a reason we simply can't understand, some of the Unchipped are unable to accept this minor detail. It goes without saying, but we won't hold anyone against their will, not at the Chip-Center or in the city itself. Our borders are open for anyone to leave or enter at any time. We don't monitor people or their whereabouts. Just like the microchipping, being part of society and everything it has to offer is one hundred percent your choice. Our system is based on freedom to choose and it always will be. We even provide electricity to those who live outside the city."

She squeezes Kaarina's hand more tightly. "But sweetheart. Listen carefully now. Considering the early state of our research, and not to forget the possible side effects of having a disconnected microchip, you must understand that staying here where we can help you is the only reasonable choice for you."

The lump in her throat makes it hard to speak. All she can do is give the doctor a nod and hope that she can continue this conversation later.

The doctor pats Kaarina's hand. "Good then. We will transfer you to the Chip-Center later today. Nurse Saarinen will stay and help you get ready." With a reassuring smile, the doctor gets up and checks the time. It surprises Kaarina to see her use something so old-fashioned as a wristwatch.

"Well, dear. I'm late for a meeting." She places her AR-glasses back on and taps the invisible control panel as she walks out of the room. Before she steps out, she turns her visor-covered face to look at Kaarina one more time.

"Don't you worry about a thing, darling. You'll be in excellent hands at the Chip-Center."

The Chip-Center is located just outside the city. It rises behind a row of apartment complexes and the kind of traditional shops that fewer and fewer people are visiting these days. Nurse Saarinen walks on the blue tiles while Kaarina walks beside her on the concrete. She dodges trash cans, charging poles, and billboards. The nurse has been talking the whole way from the hospital to the station, but Kaarina hasn't caught a word she's said.

At the front door of the Chip-Center Kaarina stops and turns to face the city.

"Why didn't we take the bus?"

"I beg your pardon?" The nurse stands by the sliding doors that keep opening and closing, confused about the object in front, not entering but not moving aside either.

"The self-driving cars. Why didn't we use them? Why the walk?"

Nurse Saarinen sighs and takes a step away from the entrance. The doors close with a soft *whoosh*.

"It's for the same reason I had you walk next to the AR-tiles and not on them. Most of your kind report severe headaches when using equipment connected to the CS."

"Okay, can you please slap this demeaning bitch so hard that she can hear the color ninety-four?"

"I'm sorry... *my kind?*" Kaarina takes a step back. The nurse winces. A nervous expression clouds her face, but only for a few seconds.

"I apologize. Let me rephrase that. For some reason individuals with a disconnected chip don't feel good when they try to use the vehicles and roads meant for the Chipped. We're in the process of fixing this. It's only a matter of time before you'll be able to use everything the city has to offer. But for now, let's stay away from the blue tiles and self-driving vehicles."

The nurse walks back to the sliding doors, holds her arm in the entrance. This time the doors stay open. A warm, amber light spills out from the hallway.

"Shall we?"

The room is decorated with soft pastel colors, with splashes of brighter color here and there. A hefty and comfortable-looking gaming chair with multiple blankets sits in the corner, opposite a queen-size bed with colorful Marimekko sheets, two pillows, and a comforter. The wallpaper is floral: red and orange tulips against a light yellow background. In the middle of the room: a round table with AR-glasses and a thick manual on top.

"Now, these may not be the latest technology, and they won't connect you with the CS." Nurse Saarinen picks up the glasses and nods at them. "But they do the job. All wellness channels are available for you to use as you wish. The 'Life Changes and Second Chances' channel is extremely popular among your ki—" Nurse Saarinen clears her throat. "Well, they're very popular around here. I highly recommend you start with that."

Kaarina drops her bag on the bed. With hesitant steps she walks to the window and looks outside. A thick line of pine trees rises in the distance. A yellow rapeseed field and a two-meter high stone wall separate the forest from the Chip-Center.

"Dinner is served at six o'clock sharp. With supper, you'll be taking your first dosage of Happiness-pills. They should help with the possible side effects you might experience after the chipping procedure." Nurse Saarinen takes out a blank medical chart and a pen, both stored on a plastic case by the door. She holds the pen in a way that makes Kaarina doubt she's ever used one in her life.

"Are you experiencing any discomfort? Headaches, sharp pain, nausea?"

Kaarina shakes her head no.

"Any abnormal sensations?"

"What do you mean?"

"Oh, I don't know." Nurse Saarinen clears her

throat again. "Like blurry vision, tinnitus or… voices?"

"This bitch is fishing. I don't trust her. They asked me the same thing today. Some bullshit about it being normal, that they can fix it. Bull. Shit. They're after our blood, our cells, whatever the fuck else we are to them. They'll probe and poke us until we're just drained sacks of meat. Don't do it girl, don't tell this hag shit."

"Miss Kaarina? Would you like us to switch back to Finnish?"

She shakes her head and meets the nurse's gaze. Continuing to speak English, she replies, "No need, I'm okay. I guess I feel a bit lightheaded, but nothing a good night's sleep wouldn't fix. I am awfully tired. Would it be possible for me to skip dinner and go straight to bed?"

The nurse puts down the chart and the pen, frowning with disappointment. She reaches for the AR-glasses and heads for the door.

"We can talk more tomorrow morning when Doctor Solomon joins us. There's a note-tablet on your nightstand. Please write down any unusual sensations and symptoms that may occur during the evening or overnight." She opens the door and waves her hand dramatically. "Ah, and here comes dinner, just in time. Why don't you eat and take the pills, maybe watch an episode of *Heal, Myself and I*?"

Someone hands the nurse a tray, which she brings to Kaarina.

"Just take the damn tray. Eat the food. But do not touch those pills."

She takes the tray from the nurse: A bowl of vegetable soup, a piece of crisp bread, two glasses of water, a pile of different shaped white pills. Nurse Saarinen's gaze drills into her, as she waits for Kaarina's reply.

Clearing her throat, Kaarina takes Bill's advice and plays along. "Better get to it then. Now that I think about it, I am famished."

The sun peeks out from between gray clouds, warm and comforting on Kaarina's face. They walk side by side next to the rapeseed field, the doctor and her. Nurse Saarinen hovers not far behind. Doctor Solomon walks slowly, her hands crossed behind her back. The doctor's calm demeanor fills Kaarina with hope. Maybe they can fix her after all? Maybe it's just a matter of days and she'll be just like everyone else—one of the Chipped?

"It's not perfect, you know," Doctor Solomon says. "The city, this world we've created. Every now and then, we get feedback, even criticism. Mostly it comes from West-Land, where life is all so different. People assume that the two regions are run under one policy. But even before The Great Affliction, this would have been impossible. People isolated themselves, created a new world inside social media, video games, and their virtual offices... Each nation lost its way, but each one in a different way."

"I'm not..." Kaarina clears her raspy throat. "I'm not sure I follow."

"Well, sweetie. Let me ask you this. How many Finns have you known to purchase a gun?"

Kaarina blinks, shakes her head.

"That's right, love. None. Even when they thought their days were numbered—and for most this was the unfortunate truth—gun violence was unheard of. Wasn't it?"

Kaarina nods.

"Then think of America, or Russia. Think of the time before. When the old world, all those troubled and muddled countries, were turned into beautifully organized cities. How people turned against one another, ready to shoot if their neighbor walked too close to their front lawn. Someone had to intervene…"

She turns and smiles at Kaarina. "Ahh, but it's such a lovely day. Too lovely for such dreary topics, don't you think?"

The doctor stops by a rosebush with flowers too colorful and vibrant to be real. Though she can't see the beauty right now, Kaarina's seen it before. Like a reflex, Kaarina's hand reaches for the AR-glasses, but she's left them in her room.

Doctor Solomon reaches for a flower, but doesn't pluck it from its bush. Instead, she leans slightly forward and presses it against her nose. Are the fake plants scented somehow? Or is the smell only there if you have a working chip?

"That plastic-sniffing dipshit. How long are you going to let this turd brainwash you?"

Kaarina doesn't answer the doctor, doesn't answer Bill. She mirrors the doctor's pose, soaking in her ease and confidence. It feels good to be so close to her, to someone who has created order in the middle of such endless chaos.

The doctor lets go of the flower, crosses her hands, and continues her slow walk. Kaarina follows, matching her footsteps with the doctor's. "Why did people kill themselves?" she can't help but ask. An image of her mother's lifeless body flashes through her mind. "I mean, I know the technology drove people to isolation. But I don't see that as a reason for suicide."

"Oh, sweetie. If only the human psyche was that easy to explain. Depression may seem simple to those who have never experienced its depth. It affects us in different ways. But one thing is for sure; if it goes untreated for too long—it'll push you under and crush you once you meet the bottom."

They've walked all the way to the stone wall that stands at the end of the Chip-Center's fenced-in yard. Nurse Saarinen stands away from them, talking into her invisible headset. With her AR-glasses on, she types fiercely into the CS Kaarina has not yet seen or used. Maybe she never will? No. She can't lose all hope. She needs to trust the system.

"And those who are in the west?" Kaarina says, thinking of the man inside her head. "What about them?"

"Hm. Well, first, their social evolution is happening

at a different speed than ours. In some places, mass-shootings, bombings, and The Race War took down the civilization extremely fast. It was bloody, chaotic, violent. People suffer from severe PTSD, panic attacks, anxiety. They remain aggressive toward other people, isolating themselves even after they're chipped and entered into the CS. Their response to the happiness-pills is slower than what we see here in the east."

"Can you believe this maniac? Trust the system.... trust my ass! The pills don't work, they never will, mostly because I ain't ever eating that shit. Kay, you gotta dump this bitch now, before she brainwashes you and turns you into one of her sheep."

Kaarina remains quiet.

"And then there's the plague. Starvation. The great fires down south. War inland. The people up north here are less aggressive, less violent toward one another. This gives us hope. We are the future."

Kaarina runs her hand on the stone wall, the damp moss ticking her fingertips. She thinks of her empty apartment in the suburbs, the horses she used to take care of at the barn not far away from her apartment. Will they make it, free and alone in the woods and fields? Or are they still at the barn, screaming their hunger, inviting predators?

"Now I'm not saying that the mass suicides our society experienced were any less devastating than the rest of The Great Affliction. But we have the right tools to control the damage. We can help this society to

74

become whole again." Doctor Solomon's smile deepens. "*You* can help, Kaarina. Talk to people, tell them to trust the system. Help them see, cooperate. All we want is for them to feel safe. Better. And they do—it's a win-win. Most understand that everything we do is for them. Their safety. Their health. Their happiness."

Doctor Solomon leans against the stone wall. The name tag on her chest pocket rises and falls to the rhythm of her calm breathing. Kaarina is overwhelmed by a sudden urge to touch her—to hold her hand or lean against her shoulder. Images of her mother flash through her mind: lying there dead on a bathroom floor, a pill bottle still resting on her palm.

After sensing that Bill has seen this painful memory, she's surprised he hasn't commented on it.

The doctor looks up at the sky, a dreamy look on her face. "Our employment level is rising. People *want* to work and participate in the city's success. Those who pedal the energy-generating bikes earn more chip credit than they can spend. Most get promoted to work at the Server-Center during their first year. Those who can't pedal work at the Vertical Farming-Center, or the Children's-Center. Our artificial insemination program is this close," she shows a small gap between her thumb and index finger, "to reversing our near-extinction."

What happens at the Children's-Center? After The Great Affliction people stopped reproducing. Most chose to live alone without a partner or even friends–assuming they had any left. Her mother once told her it wouldn't be too long until people wouldn't even be able to reproduce. Whether they wanted to or not. Kaarina wants to ask the doctor about this, but she's completely tongue-tied.

"The latest happiness research shows that people are more content than they've been since The Great Affliction. They've started to talk to one another again, building trust in the goodness of humankind. The chipping and the Happiness-Program has lifted us from the brink of extinction back to being an organized and coping society—dare I say, a successful society."

The doctor spreads her hands, gives a little laugh. "The Pedal-Center threw their first annual party just the other week. They had a dance competition, can you believe it? Many employees of the Center participated. Everyone had cake and apple juice. The whole city is still talking about it. One day, sweetie, you'll be part of this cheer."

Tiny letters stand out on one of the stones. For a reason she can't quite understand, Kaarina doesn't want to lean over to read the carving. She fingers the surface, trying to feel out the carved message. *Juokse pois tästä paikasta.* It's her native language.

"What does it mean, Kay?"

Careful not to talk to her new-found psychic friend out loud, Kaarina communicates with him with silent words. *It says, "Run from this place."*

"See? I told you, I knew it. Your world is not any different from mine. It's corrupt, wrong. You do need to run, to leave before—"

"And as fascinating and important as our history is, we're here to talk about *you* and *your* future. Which is bright, by the way, did I mention that already? Yes, my dear, you are extremely lucky to be here. The Chip-Center is one of the most successful facilities we have. All its tenants have everything they could possibly ask for. No need to leave the facility. Nurse Saarinen gave you the applications, right, sweetie?"

Kaarina thinks of the stack of papers next to her AR-glasses on the table in her room. Nurse Saarinen did give them to her: she had placed them on the tray in a plastic folder, tucked under the dinner plate and a mountain of pills. She had finished her meal but flushed the pills down the toilet as soon as Nurse Saarinen had exited her room.

"I'm afraid I haven't had a chance to look at the papers just yet."

The doctor's smile reaches her eyes. She places her hand on Kaarina's shoulder, gives it a pleasant squeeze. "You take all the time you need, dear. The Unchipped are special, *you* are special. There's no need for rushing. Eat, rest. Let the pills balance your mind and body. Enjoy the wellness channels. We've got all the time in the world."

"But don't I need to work? To earn my keep?"

Her laughter is soft, soothing. "Ah, what did I tell you? Honest, hardworking, and loyal. You truly are a model citizen of East-Land. Don't rush, you have the rest of your life to pedal that bike. The only thing you need to do is check in at the lab. They'll take a few quick tests, just the standard procedure so we can make sure the chipping left you in good health. The rest will come when the time is right."

A muffled scream echoes from the direction of the Chip-Center. Nurse Saarinen starts, makes a short swipe at the air with one hand, and takes off her AR-glasses. Hurried and edgy, she taps the doctor on her shoulder. "Laura, I think it's time to get back now."

"Was that someone screaming?" Kaarina says, her eyes wide at the sudden sound.

Doctor Solomon's eyes never leave Kaarina's. It's like she's oblivious to their surroundings, one hundred percent focused on Kaarina and her well being. "A scream?" she chuckles a little. "I didn't hear anything of the sort. Did you, Nurse Saarinen?"

The nurse forces a smile and shakes her head.

"The main fan on the Chip server has been making this high-pitched noise for the last two days." One more squeeze of Kaarina's shoulder sends a warm sensation through Kaarina's body. She's safe, she can feel it. So why can't her gut get with the program?

"I must get back to the lab now. Make sure you stop by before dinner is served. I will be there and will personally take your blood sample. Because you are special, Kaarina, and I feel very connected to you. You'll be such a great success here at the Chip-Center and later on in the city."

Then she lets go of Kaarina's shoulders, turns

around, and follows Nurse Saarinen back into the building.

Kaarina kneels down to investigate the stone wall more closely. Her fingers find another carving, this one smaller than the first one. "*Katso laatikon ulkopuolelle.*"

"*Does it say "Doctor Solomon can suck it?"*

No, it does not.

"*Then what does it say?*"

Kaarina stands up and looks at the tree line rising across the field. A shadow moves in the woods, then disappears into the gloom before she can tell if it was a deer or a person or a hallucination. The blanket of clouds covers the sun. Arms wrapped around her Chip-Center jacket, she shivers and stares at the tree line longingly.

"*Kay? What does the damn carving say?*"

"It says to think outside the box."

CHAPTER 4
AMONG THE SHEEP

Kaarina walks into the remote part of the city, her socks damp but not soaked in her summer sandals. She hasn't found her shoe, but would look again on her way back. She sits down on the frost-covered park bench, shifting restlessly from side to side.

The crooked pharmacy sign is unlit. No blue suits stroll down the blue tile road. The moon shines its weak yellow light through the wispy clouds. It's too early to be here. She knew it would be, but she couldn't stop herself from running through the woods and back into the city as quickly as she could.

Leaving Rocky alone at the barn made her chest hurt. If the Yeti and his black market crew were to come back, the gelding wouldn't stand a chance. Yesterday, Rocky's fight against the uninvited visitors had saved his life, but it had also sapped his energy and worsened his infection. It might be too late, even if Kaarina could somehow succeed in tracking down Markus and getting another batch of antibiotics. And food. Her stomach aches when she thinks of her nightly crisp bread.

But how is she to find Markus? Knocking on the Chipped's doors would be the quickest way to get the attention of the guards. To get her on the troublemaker list.

Going into the pharmacy herself is not an option either. The building glows with blue light because it's connected to the city's CS. It would shock her until she passed out or even died. It's hard to tell what the blue light would do to her in the long run; she's never tried to find out.

She's stuck on this park bench. Sitting in the dim blue light. Waiting.

She taps her foot on the concrete ground. When the wind picks up, she tightens her hoodie strings to protect her neck and forehead from the icy breeze. The humming of the tile road fills her ears. Both sandals now tap rapidly against the hard ground.

When the park lights flicker on, blue light mixing with yellow, Kaarina jumps up. It's almost morning. She paces around the bench.

Markus lives here, in this part of the city, but there's more than one road leading to the downtown area and the Server-Center where he works. She'll need to catch him before he gets there. Just a quick pop into the pharmacy, maybe one or two vegan granola bars, that's all she'll ask. She'll pay him later–next week, or even tomorrow. Hell, she'll spend a day with him if that's what it takes, but it has to be later. Do the Chipped get days off from work? Which days? Are Sundays still a thing?

A tall building rises in the distance. In the field next to it, long rapeseed stems sway slowly in the wind. It's been two years since she ran away from the Chip-Center. While she stands and stares at the building, memories flash through her anxious mind like a surgeon's knife.

Nurse Saarinen kneeling by the toilet, emptying a white lump of flushed-down, half-melted pills from a secret strainer.

Doctor Solomon's soft and reassuring voice, telling her how she understands.

Her own bare feet, flapping against the concrete sidewalks.

The stabbing pain whenever she crosses the blue tiles, getting closer to the woods.

Bill's frantic voice, screaming at her to run faster.

She never filled out the applications. She never pedaled a bike or grew a potato or bottle-fed a newborn baby. She never met with the other Unchipped in the center—the other test subjects, *her kind*.

Her week in the Chip-Center was divided between the lab and her room. Doctor Solomon drew blood, asked about weird sensations, voices or hallucinations. Nurse Saarinen told her what channels to watch, what food to eat, what pills to take. Somehow, every day, she was able to get away with not doing the latter.

On the last day of her brief visit, she refused to be

plugged into a brain scanner. They told her she'd be "out cold for only a split second". Bill screamed "*scam, scam, scam, scam,*" for so long, she was finally too anxious to co-operate. She was sent back to her room.

That night the nurses paid her a surprise visit. Nurse Saarinen made a beeline for her tiny bathroom, knelt by the toilet and pulled out the flushed pills.

Before the dumbfounded nurses had time to react, Kaarina ran through the door, down the hall, and into the city. Maybe they didn't care if she stayed or went—no one ever followed her out of the Chip-Center.

Through the city and through the woods, Kaarina had run to her old apartment. There she found that most of her belongings were gone, scavenged by the outcasts—people like her.

Collecting anything she could fit in a torn plastic bag, Kaarina had gathered together a pair of jeans, two stained T-shirts, her worn-out sneakers, her never-worn summer sandals, and a fleece lined hoodie, tucked away at the back of the closet.

The plastic bag slung over her shoulder, she walked thirty minutes until she was at the barn where she used to work. All the stalls were empty and the aisle was cluttered with broken buckets, empty grain bags, and ripped-apart horse blankets.

The hay loft above the barn was untouched. After arranging the hay bales into a single bed, she used the manure-stained horse blankets to keep herself warm, hiding her few belongings under the loose floorboards.

There she waited for the Chipped to arrive.

Days crept by. The few small stores—only a five-minute walk away—were the only places she visited. There, she ate what crispbread and canned beans she could find and carried the rest up to the hay loft.

At nighttime she waited—for them. For her forced return to the city.

But they never came.

Flabbergasted, she had questioned her own sanity. Why on earth had she run away? Only an idiot would choose not to stay and let them fix whatever was wrong with her brain.

During the months that followed, she let Bill reassure her that lying low and keeping watch was the right course of action. But the city kept pulling her back. It still tempts her today, even if its buildings and roads make her ill. She wants to be like the rest of them: content, snug, filled with possibilities. But just the thought of taking one of their pills, or jumping into the program with two feet, images of her mother rush right back into her mind. Something about her suicide doesn't add up. The pills, scattered around her—

An electric buzz interrupts her reminiscence and makes her turn around: the pharmacy sign is back on. The front door opens, and an old man with a hunched back walks out. He seems to be walking straight at her, standing behind the park bench.

AR-glasses hanging from one hand, a familiar-looking paper bag from the other, the man makes his way across the pavement and the blue tiles. He stops in front of the park bench.

His visor pointed at the Chip-Center rising in the distance, the man stares into space, silently. Can't he see Kaarina standing there?

A deep sigh fills the air between them. The man places the paper bag on the park bench, sits down next to it. Kaarina's frozen on her feet, unsure what to do.

"What kind of infection is it?"

She cocks her head, takes a step closer.

"What?"

"Your horse, what kind of an infection does it have? Considering the amount of medicine the young man purchased for you yesterday, it's a horse you're trying to save. Unless you've made friends with the moose or the bears…" He stops to laugh a little at his own joke, "But that's unlikely, considering that you're standing there in one piece."

With careful steps, Kaarina walks around the bench and sits on the opposite side from him. He must have seen her through the pharmacy window yesterday. How else would he know it was her who Markus bought the medicine for?

"It's something in his respiratory system. He can barely breathe."

The man takes off his AR-glasses, exposing a glazed eye. His other eye is only partly covered by the milky film.

"Your eye," Kaarina says, knowing that she shouldn't stare. Or ask. "Can't they fix it?"

"They sure can."

"But?"

A shrug. The man gives her a small smile. "I rather know when it's my time to go. Let my body age with dignity. Not all of us have the need to run from what's coming."

The paper bag rustles as he places it between them on the bench. He nods toward it, his hands playing with the headband on his AR-glasses.

Kaarina holds her breath, hesitating, her eyes moving between the old man and the paper bag between them.

"What's in the bag?"

"All the antibiotics I have left in the store. It's not like anyone else is coming for them. You can have them and use them as you wish. My wife, bless her heart, had horses all her life. I wish I could tell you they didn't end up on the black market. That I somehow saved them before I moved away from our farm and into the city."

"I'm sorry to hear that."

He shrugs. A halfhearted smile crosses his face. "I guess that's not my biggest regret. I wish I did a lot of things. And left some undone."

"Don't we all, grandpa. Don't we all."

Kaarina reaches for the bag, opens it to peek in: At least thirty pill boxes, enough to cure Rocky three times over, if it ever came to it. The man sighs again.

"I should have seen it coming. She withered away to nothing, shying away from me and even from Toni. My wife was always so upbeat, so full of life. Not a cranky stress ball, not like me. I should have gotten help when she changed, instead of telling her to cheer up and snap out of it."

When the images of her mother, dead in the middle of the ocean of pills, rush through her mind, Kaarina lets go of the bag and places her hand on his. Tears fill his half-blind eyes. Back hunched on the bench, it seems as he's trying to wrap himself into a tiny ball and roll away from life.

"What was her name?"

Surprise shadows his face, but only for a second. His eyes search for hers; his back straightens an inch.

"Helena. Hm."

His warm smile vanishes as quickly as it appears.

"And Toni was your son?"

"Is… Toni is our son. He got stuck in West-Land during The Great Affliction. Someone told me he's living with the Unchipped somewhere in City of California. I would give anything to hear from him, just to know he's okay, that he's breathing."

He has to stop and clear his throat before continuing.

"I didn't do much with my life, but Toni is something I did right. Something I can be proud of. I never had the guts to travel, let alone move abroad. I became a pharmacist because my father was a pharmacist. I married my high school sweetheart, because that's what my parents did as well. I worked from eight 'til four, all my life, because I always assumed that's what you're supposed to do. Toni and my Helena were all I had, but they were enough. With both of them gone, I didn't have anything left." He looks at her. "But I'm not letting them plug me in one of their capsules," he says sternly. "Not until I know my Toni is okay out there."

Bill? Are you hearing this? Bill?

"If I only knew he was okay, maybe I could forgive myself."

Her eyes fixed on the old man, Kaarina continues her silent search for Bill. *You could look for him, ask around. Maybe you can even tap him?*

Bill's sigh reveals his presence. *"Yeah, sure I can. We all know that the Unchipped are trusting and social people. They'll let any stranger tap them, no questions asked."*

Kaarina blinks to stop herself from rolling her eyes. *Could you just once agree to something, without being such a dick?*

"Oh I'm the dick? Just because you've started some sort of an escort service in your little digi-village, doesn't mean that I can do the same."

What if I asked nicely?

"That would be a first."

Please, Bill. I'll owe you one. Anything you need.

When Bill stops arguing with her, she knows he has given up. Bill will help her find the old man's missing son. Kaarina gives him a half-smile. "Listen, sir…"

"It's Raino. Just call me Raino."

"Okay, Raino. I can't tell you exactly how, but I might be able to help. I'll have someone look for your son in City of California. I can't promise you they'll find him, but we can at least try."

"Oh, so that's how it's going to be? A dick and an errand boy?

The old man's face lightens up. His posture straightens in front of her, eyes still teary but now filled with hope. He holds onto Kaarina's hands, squeezes them hard, leans forward and says, "That's all I need. All I ever wanted."

"You said something about them plugging you in a capsule? What does that mean?"

Raino slumps again, but he doesn't let go of her hands. "We're not supposed to talk about it, I think. Not that any of us really talk to one another about anything anymore. Maybe about the gloomy weather. But that's it."

"You're not supposed to talk about what?"

He lets go of her hands to fidget with the headband again. Hands shaking, maybe because of his old age, maybe because of this forbidden conversation, he looks away from Kaarina. Their conversation is over.

Blue suits emerge from the nearby apartment building. The old man stands up, takes the paper bag and places it on Kaarina's lap.

"I must go now. People may not talk to one another, but they're loyal to the city. They'll go to the guards if they see any suspicious activity. I don't want to risk my deal with them."

He places the AR-glasses on his head. "I'll look for you, through the window. If you hear from my son, you know where to find me. Next time I see you, I'll have another paper bag for you. No—I'll have two paper bags. All the medicine you and your equine friend may need."

Kaarina hesitates, but only for a second.

"Sir… Raino. I don't need more medicine. But my food stock could really use some filling."

The old man digs into his pocket and pulls out three vegan granola bars. He places them in Kaarina's hands, holds them firmly.

"They may taste like mouthwash, but here. I'll have more for you when we meet again."

"Did I leave you with any? Here," Kaarina hands back one of the bars, "Two is enough to get me back home. There's Yellowfoots left in the woods. I'll figure it out."

He shakes his head to the bar Kaarina's offering him. "And here I thought the Unchipped eat better than we do. I still dream about bacon and eggs every night."

Kaarina shoves the bars in her pocket.

Raino stops to think, and then says, "If you need more food… This connection you have. Can you search for other missing persons? In addition to my son?"

This is it. The opportunity. Her new food supply. But is she giving a promise she can't possibly keep?

"I could look for others. Yes."

Before he leaves, Raino says, "Give me a day or two.

Let me talk to my people. I'll make sure next time you visit the city, you won't leave with an empty stomach."

A virtual dog walker strolls down the blue tiles. When he passes the old man, now crossing the tile road to get back to his pharmacy, he turns his head slightly, pretends not to notice him. Kaarina watches, puzzled. How does the social ranking even work—the thing Markus is so scared to lose—if no one is willing to acknowledge anyone else's existence?

The old man makes his way back under the crooked pharmacy sign. He opens the door, disappears inside. There he'll wait by the window for her to return.

Kaarina takes off running. She's been here for too long. The city and its lights have slowly drilled into her bones, gnawing little holes into her muscles and sending throbbing pain through her skull.

While walking, she digs out a vegan bar and unwraps it. While biting into its tasteless core, she does her best to celebrate her new source of food. But at the same time, something else turns her stomach. Regret. Doubt. She'll have all the food she can eat while she waits for her big move back into the city. But what do those feeding her get? Is she turning into a scam artist? Taking advantage of an old man and his innocent friends?

Is she just as shameless as the rest of the Unchipped?

Dust, horsehair, and wood shavings fly around her head. The curry comb moves in circles over Rocky's back, leaving its round markings on his thick winter coat. Kaarina bangs the comb against the barn floor, to clear off the mud and dirt stuck between the rubber teeth.

"So yeah, your guy has quite the operation going up there." Bill's been going on about the pharmacist's son for some time now. *"And it's not just the Unchipped he takes care of in his little underground clinic. Turns out his medical services are quite popular among the Chipped as well."*

"So, Toni is a doctor?"

"Not just any doctor. He was one of the best ones in San Diego, before the Happiness Program. But get this, it gets even wilder. One of the Unchipped that let me tap them told me Toni's not even Unchipped. I mean he doesn't have a chip, but that's because he never tried to get one in the first place."

"He volunteered to live outside the city? Why would anyone do that?"

"Why not? I don't mind this lifestyle. It's kinda growing on me."

"That's because you live in a palace with all the food you can eat and all the boy toys you can dream of."

"Jealous much, Kay-Kay?"

Kaarina can't help but smile. Now that she knows she'll have food coming in and possibly a new pair of winter boots, it's easier to be kind to Bill. To take his know-it-all-ness for what it is: friendly teasing.

Rocky turns to groom her back, his muzzle tickling

the back of Kaarina's neck. She stops the currycombing and scratches the inside of his ear instead. Five days of antibiotics and there's no sign of the infection.

"Who knows what goodies you'll get out of this. I'm telling you, this escort service of yours could be a real moneymaker."

"It's not an escort service. Stop saying that."

"Get more meds, Kay. That'll keep Yeti and his witches happy. They may have all the food they need, but medical supply is a whole new ballgame. They'll surely lay off your animals and leave you be."

She kneels down and selects a hoof pick from the damaged grooming kit. The Unchipped not paying her another visit is nerve-wracking. Why hasn't the leader come back for more? Joining their community is not an option, not if she wants to protect the animals at the barn. But maybe bringing them supplies will get them off her back.

Tomorrow's the day when she's supposed to meet Markus in the city. She'll make him laugh and feel better. Then she'll visit the old man's pharmacy. If Raino's found Kaarina more missing persons to track, she can only hope they'll be within her or Bill's reach. Not many Unchipped agree to help someone they don't know. But she has to try. Or before she knows it, she'll need to beg for food.

Maybe Kaarina can find a local Unchipped to try tapping with? To find an ally somewhere in the suburbs?

"Oh, so this escort business is not enough for you?" Of

course Bill's still there. Listening, snooping. *"Well you know what they say: keep your friends close and your Yetis even closer."*

"That's the plan, Bill."

"If a Yeti doesn't come to Muhammad, Muhammad must go to the Yeti."

"That's cute."

"Fear makes the Yeti bigger than he is."

"Mm-hm."

"Don't let the fear of the Yeti keep you from playing the game."

"Bill?"

"Yah?"

"Go find your own toy to play with."

Heavy rain has turned the dirt road into a muddy stream. Above the wall, a blue glow reflects off of the humidity in the air. The blue suits that walk near the entrance all carry enormous bright-blue umbrellas, staying dry in the downpour.

Doctor Solomon once told her that the augmented reality provides perfect weather, three hundred and sixty-five days a year. Snow melts whenever it falls too close to the buildings, which radiate heat as well as blue light. She wonders what the Chipped see when it rains. Rainbows? Sun showers? The pressing need to know, to see what the others see, makes Kaarina's stomach twist.

As she gets closer to the wall, her heart skips a beat.

Two guards stand by the main entrance, staring right at her. Usually, they turn their blank faces away. Act like she's invisible. That is, if the guards are even around. Attacks or bomb threats in the city are almost unheard of these days.

Should she turn around, run away? The guards would catch her in no time, with their electric cars or scooters or eagle-sized drones. Maybe her suspicious behavior would get her shot down, the muddy stream her final resting place.

The guards, motionless, patiently wait for her to stop in front of them. Rain has turned her clothes into wet rags, but the water slides off the guards' waterproof uniforms.

The younger and flimsier of the two guards clears his throat.

"Good day, Miss Kaarina. We are here to escort you to see Doctor Solomon at the Chip-Center. Apparently, she has some good news to share with you today. If you wouldn't mind following us, please."

Pulse strong in her chest, her blood rushing in her ears, Kaarina stares at the blue men, digesting their message.

"Laura wants to see me? What for?"

"We don't know what the news is, Miss." The other guard—five, maybe ten years older than his colleague—shrugs halfheartedly. "We're only here to tell you that this is a time sensitive invitation. And that your time is running out. Would you be so kind as to step into the vehicle? It'll get us out of the rain and into the Chip-Center quicker than walking."

Bill? What is this?

"Whatever you do, do not *get into that car, Kay."*

She nods, more to Bill than the guards. "I'm afraid I can't get in your vehicle. Not without feeling like I have a nail pounding through my brain. It's okay, I don't mind walking. I'll just meet the doctor once I get there."

"Do not go to the center. It's a trap, you know it is."

Relax. I got this.

The older guard walks up to her, gently leading her through the entrance and inside the city. "You'll be able to sit in this one."

An old gray Volvo stands by the wall. Kaarina hasn't seen a gasoline-powered vehicle since the inception of the Happiness Program.

What if she did it—what if she climbed into the backseat? Why does the doctor want to see her now, after two years without anyone ever coming after her? Could her research team have figured it out? Kaarina's damaged brain?

The younger guard opens the back door, waits for her to get in. The leather seating inside look flawless. A new car smell reaches her nose.

She hesitates, talks to Bill silently. *It can't be a new car, can it? And why do they have cars specifically for Unchipped now? I thought they all got destroyed because of the pollution.*

"Oh, that's what we're worried about right now?

Climate change? Walk away Kay, I'm not going to tell you again. Something's not right. This is fishy as fuck."

"Miss? Let's get you out of the rain." The older man places his hand back on her shoulder and gives her a push. This time the gesture is not as careful and or as friendly. Kaarina dodges his touch, takes three sidesteps.

"I said, I do not mind walking. And I don't mind the rain. Besides, I have someone to see. Just tell Doctor Solomon I'll stop by on my way out."

The lie flows too easily, like she means it. But meeting Solomon would be a foolish thing to do; nothing she says can be trusted. At the same time, Kaarina can't push the thought out of her mind that Doctor Solomon might have found a way to connect her chip to the CS. It powers its way back into her brain. Tempting, alluring.

What if they did it? What if a broken brain can now be fixed?

They're watching her. Maybe through cameras, maybe drones, she's not sure. But she can feel the burning sensation of an intense stare.

Instead of the park bench, she heads straight to the crooked sign, to Raino's pharmacy. The blue lights blaze in the darkening afternoon. No blue suits are around. The pathways around the apartment complex are empty and even the park seems gloomier than it did before.

Three careful knocks on the window, and the door opens. Glazed, blurry eyes peek out, then look left and right, like someone about to cross a busy road.

"Come on in."

"I can't. The blue light in your shop will make me sick."

His head disappears, but the door stays open a crack. Soon the crooked sign goes off. So do the lights inside the pharmacy. Raino glances back outside.

"Not if the power's shut down. Come on, there's someone I'd like you to meet."

A dozen lit candles greet her as she walks inside. The door closes silently behind them. From the dark corners, muffled whispers reach her ears, along with the sounds of people moving around restlessly. But Kaarina can't see anyone other than Raino.

The old pharmacist walks to the counter, picks up a black backpack, and brings it over to Kaarina. His AR-glasses are nowhere to be seen. The bag is heavy, bursting at the seams.

"It's from all of us. Not just medicine, but clothing, dry food, lotions, hand warmers, and a pair of brand-new winter boots. Never used."

"But I haven't even told you about Toni yet."

He smiles and reaches for her hands. The touch is warm, genuine. It sends her back to the way things were before, when people still had enough trust to touch one another. No wonder Markus had been so moved when he touched her face.

"I know, I know. And if you have news for me, that's wonderful. But if you don't, you are still going to keep the bag. We don't need any of it. With those antibiotics, you chose to help someone who can never repay you. Now, we're doing the same."

A lump tickles her throat. She swallows back the tears and rapidly blinks her eyes.

In the candlelight, five, maybe more people make their way forward with soft steps. Ten. Who are they? Is she in danger?

She swings the bag onto her back, ready for anything. The blue suits in front of her stand still, staring.

"Where is your escort boy?"

What?

"Where's your lover boy? Check that bag Kay, nobody's generous just to be nice. Could be a scam."

Food and meds, that's what's in the bag. I'm sure of it.

In her mind's eye, she sees Bill wave his hands in frustration. A margarita glass tips over, spilling half its contents on a white tile floor.

She returns her attention to Raino. "Your son runs an underground medical clinic in City of California. He helps the Unchipped to survive outside the city. My... source tells me he's such a great doctor that some of the Chipped prefer to see him instead of using the city services. Toni's doing amazing, Mister Raino. Your son is a hero."

Tears fill his milky eyes. His face lights up, making him look years younger than he did just a moment ago.

A soft sound escapes his throat, something Kaarina can't make sense of at first. Something he's clearly not used to, either.

His laughter fills the room.

The old man sits down on the chair by the counter. The black backpack heavy on her shoulders, Kaarina watches as the blue-suited shadows start creeping closer.

A woman, maybe her age or a few years younger, steps up to her and reaches for her hands.

"Markus told me you make people feel good. How do you do it? Do you have any lucky charms I could purchase from you? I'll give you anything, I have a lot of CC's." Her eyes move rapidly between Kaarina's eyes, like she thinks she'll find an answer there—a meaning to her life.

"You... you don't need to buy me any more things, I have all I need for now. I can, um... listen? If you want to tell me what's bothering you?"

"What, you're an escort and *a therapist?"*

Shut up, shut up, shut up. I can't just ditch her.

The woman moves closer and half-whispers. "The thing is, I'm not sure what's wrong with me. I've already talked to my doctor in the city. He prescribed me the latest happiness-pills and I guess they're helping a little. I sleep better. I sleep a lot."

Kaarina grabs her hands and nods to tell her to keep talking.

"I have everything I need, all the trendy AR-clothes and accessories. I'm not lying, I've got them all. I work at the Server-Center where they plug me in for eight hours every day. I get more CC's than I need without even noticing that I've worked that day. It's like a nap and you're done working. I have three digital dogs, a house, an AR-partner that is more than wonderful and faithful—"

"Wait, an AR-partner? Like a robot?" Kaarina looks around and sees the blue suits smiling. Her words amuse them. Carefully, they glance around to see if others have heard the joke as well. Are they afraid to laugh? Why?

"Oh, you're funny. No, not a robot. An AR-partner in the augmented reality. So we wouldn't have to live alone. I'm signed up for my first insemination in only two weeks. I'm telling you, my life is perfect."

Eyes wide, Kaarina stares at the woman. "Well, as long as you're happy with your life. I guess I'm not sure what I can do to help?"

The woman squeezes her hands. "I guess..." she looks over her shoulder. Leaning in, she whispers in Kaarina's ear, "I guess I just need some extra luck, to keep all of this going. Maybe I'm feeling like... like this, because I'm afraid I'll lose it all. What if one day I'm not happy anymore?"

Shaking her head, Kaarina lets out a small chuckle. "Happy? You think you're *happy*? Listen, you need to talk to people, touch them, hang out with them. And not through the AR-glasses, but face to face. Stop dodging one another on the street. When's the last time you told someone a secret? The last time you kissed someone? Slept with someone?"

But when's the last time Kaarina herself did all this? Any of this? Moving into the city was always supposed to be the cure, but now it sounds as it's the same sickness, only with different symptoms. At least in the woods, out there alone, she can decide for herself.

"I do those things with Mike every night…. He is programmed to—"

"No, no, no, no. I'm not talking about some hologram you bought to spend the rest of your life with. A real person."

Her eyes wander to their hands, holding each other tight. Kaarina's fingernails are blackened by muck and dirt from the barn. A faint smell of horse and hay lingers around them.

"When's the last time you danced? Flirted with someone? Told them a joke?"

The woman's head snaps back, as if in surprise. Eyes flickering, she stares at Kaarina.

"Knock, knock."

"Holy flaming monkey balls. Is this really happening?"

Kaarina smiles at the woman. "Who's there?"

"Spell."

"Spell who?"

"Okay, okay: W.H.O."

The joke is too ridiculous for Kaarina to do anything but laugh. When she giggles, the blue suits around them shift their weight from one foot to another. Raino's chuckles softly by the counter.

Suddenly, the woman gives her a bear hug.

"Thank you, Miss. I have a friend that I used to see before... before all this. You remind me of her. We haven't seen each other since we left the suburbs, but I know she lives near me. Maybe I should—"

"Yes, please, go see her. Digi-Mike can survive one night without you."

A young man in a blue suit moves closer. "What about me? I don't know anyone here, my only friends were my football teammates. They all died during The Great Affliction. Our team kept losing and they... they just couldn't take it. Who do I tell jokes to?"

An older lady with a gray poncho wrapped around her blue suit steps forward. She grabs Kaarina's sleeve and pulls on it. "My daughter lives in City of England. I can't reach her. We haven't talked since the boats stopped. You have to find out where she is. You need to tell me she's okay."

A middle-aged man pushes the woman with the poncho aside and grabs Kaarina's shoulders. "I heard you have a rabbit foot for sale? I'll give you fifty CC's for it, right now."

The room starts spinning as the blue suits appear from the shadows, touching her, pulling her, talking, requesting, demanding. Kaarina folds her arms across her belly and tries to step away. Raino's gentle voice asks people to calm down, but his demand is drowned out by the frantic chattering.

The front door to the pharmacy opens.

Markus barges into the middle of the circle, wraps his arm around Kaarina. "Hey, hey, hey, let go of her. Let her…" He pulls her away and quickly walks her out the door.

No one follows them. Once the front door closes, the crooked sign lights up and the hum of electricity fills their ears. Has it always been this loud?

"Sorry about that. About them. I guess I'm not the only one who's been waiting to see you."

Kaarina shoves her hands into her pockets. Smiling, she looks away from Markus. "You've waited to see me?"

Markus laughs a bit and then turns his face away too. "I, umm…I guess—"

"I've waited to see you too," Kaarina says, putting Markus out of his misery. He smiles and exhales, clearly relieved. In comfortable silence, they walk together along the blue tiles. Blue suits walk by them. As usual, they look the other way, as if Kaarina doesn't exist.

"So you found Toni?"

"I did."

"Are you able to tell me how?" His smile is careful, as is his voice.

Kaarina bites her lip. How could she explain any of it to him? Bill, the connection between them? How is she to explain something she doesn't understand herself?

"Maybe I'll tell you the next time we meet?"

Markus stops and looks at her. His blue eyes investigate Kaarina's face. "I like that plan," he says, and turns to continue his slow stroll . The low hum of the city is the only sound in their ears as they continue along in silence. Soon, they're standing near the Chip-Center, rising unnaturally white against the gloomy sky.

Kaarina nods toward the front door of the building. "Did you know that Doctor Solomon sent her men to pick me up from the gates today?"

Frowning, Markus considers her words before replying. "Why does the head of the Chip-Center want to see you?"

Kaarina stares at the building in front of them. No blue light reflects from its white brick wall, no electricity hums nearby.

"Do not even think about it."

"Well, I'm thinking maybe… Maybe they figured it out? My brain… maybe she knows how to connect the chip properly."

Markus stays quiet for a moment, clearly pondering his words. "Is that what you really want? To become Chipped? What about your animals? And all your adventures?"

"It's not really that kind of a life, Markus." She hears the edge in her tone, but can't help it. "You've romanticized it."

Markus bites his thumbnail. "It's not always that great in the city, either, you know. What if you've got it all wrong?"

"The blue-boy's onto something. That doctor has always been bad news. You ran from her once already, don't you

remember? The pills, the isolation… it's a mind-fuck, nothing more and nothing less."

Kaarina frowns and answers Bill silently. *The Chip-Center is not the same as the city. Being Chipped is not the same as being Unchipped. Don't you get that? If they can fix me, it'll change everything. I'll finally fit in."*

Bill scoffs, flustered, but doesn't continue their argument.

Doesn't she deserve a simple life? Does everything need to be so damn difficult? Just because her brain is malfunctioning and somehow wrong. Still, why should she have to live alone? So what if she'd give in. Let them decide what she'll eat, when she'll sleep, who she's to talk with. So what? At least she won't starve to death, rotting in some moldy barn that even the animals have abandoned.

After two careful steps toward the center, Kaarina stops and clenches her hands into fists. Or maybe Bill is right. This is foolish. Reckless. Idiotic. She should stay away, live with what she's got. Enjoy the food and the safe place she lives. She rolls her eyes at herself. Hah, 'safe'. And when's the last time she's enjoyed any of the food she's eaten? But what about Markus? At least she should find out if he would actually stick around. He may be Chipped but there's no question in Kaarina's mind about whether he can be trusted. Her life as Unchipped has improved. Everything will be okay.

"Kaarina? Hello? What if you're wrong about this?"

She lifts her chin, looking over Markus' shoulder. "I

guess there's only one way to find out."

"Oh, hell no. No, no, no."

Markus shakes his head while Bill continues his objections.

She waves them both off. "I just want to know. Whether they figured it out or not. I'll just pop in and come right back out. That's all. What's the harm in gaining information?

The black backpack swings from side to side as she walks in the Chip-Center's front door, Bill's furious shouts filling her brain.

The Chip-Center meeting room makes her wish she still had access to her old bedroom, the one with yellow and red flowered wallpaper and designer sheets. While she sits on the white couch, Markus paces around the room, his hands deep in his blue overall pockets.

"I have a bad feeling about this," he says, marching around the sitting area. Then he stops and looks at his wrist, where Kaarina sees nothing but a blue sleeve. Markus places the AR-glasses briefly on his face, peers at his wrist again. "I really should be at work."

"What? Some friend you have here. He's going to leave? Now? Might as well throw you to the wolves. Cut you open for them, even."

He's not my friend, Bill. And therefore he's under no obligation to stay. He just felt bad for me when he saw those people harassing me at Raino's place, so he helped me out.

107

Markus has picked up his pace. He circles the low coffee table in the middle of the seating area. After each round, he stops, picks up his glasses, checks the time, changes direction and keeps circling the table. After his fifth round, Kaarina jumps up from her seat.

"Stop. You're making me dizzy. And we're not in a time-capsule here. You don't need to check the time every thirty seconds. Just go to work, I'll be fine. I'll come back next week and we can talk. I'll tell you then what Laura wanted." She doesn't mean to be short with him. So snappy. But her shredded nerves seem to have wiped out her manners. Maybe she's more nervous than she thought.

Markus cocks his head to one side. "Who's Laura?"

"I mean Doctor Solomon. Who knows? Maybe it's good news. Maybe next time you see me I'll be one of you guys. I can walk the blue tiles, watch crappy wellness shows, and work at the Server-Center with you and Raino. We'll be one big happy family."

"That's unlikely. Raino can't work in the Server-Center, they have an age limit. He can keep his pharmacy job, or he can retire. That's it."

"You're wrong, he can work at the Server-Center. He told me he'd let them plug him in as soon as he knew that Toni was alive."

Markus freezes in place. His AR-glasses slip from his hands. They hit the floor with a *bang* that echoes through the small room. "Did he really say that? They told him they'd plug him in?"

"Yeah, in a capsule of some sort. That's what he says."

"You're one hundred percent sure about that?"

"I am sure. It's not like he's a man of many words."

"Kaarina, that's not right at all. That means these people—"

The meeting room door flies open, interrupting Markus's hasty words. He turns to see Doctor Solomon and two nurses, who all walk in with friendly smiles on their faces. Then, four men and three women, all dressed in matching blue uniforms, enter the room. Kaarina's never seen them before. They nod at her, stand by the entryway with their arms folded on the front of their blue overalls. Do they live in the center? Or are they Laura's bodyguards? Why are there so many people suddenly present?

Markus turns his back on them, shakes his head rapidly, and whispers, "You don't need to decide anything right now, Kaarina. Raino and I will help you. You'll have food, friends. I promise. Just don't agree to anything they suggest. Not today."

"Ah, Kaarina. So wonderful to see you again. It's been—what—two years since you left us and the Center? I'm so sorry about the way we left things, but I'm glad to see you back here."

She meets the doctor's warm eyes and smiles back at her. The same calming sensation Kaarina remembers from their walks around the facility comes over her. The doctor makes her feel welcome and wanted.

"This bitch is up to no good. Listen to Markus, Kay. Walk. Away."

Doctor Solomon turns to Markus, raises her eyebrows. "And Mister Nyman, to what do we owe this pleasure? Have you left your new position at the Server-Center? We had such great hopes for you and that house you picked out on the west side of the city. Such gorgeous interior design!"

Markus blinks rapidly, his voice shaking slightly as he replies. "I'm still at the Server-Center, Ma'am. Just helping Kaarina find her way around the city."

"A gentleman, then, hmm? Isn't that lovely." The doctor looks at the two nurses next to her. They nod enthusiastically along with her words. "But I can assure you that Kaarina is perfectly safe. After all, she's found her way back to me. And what news do I have for you today! Tell me, dear, are you ready for a long-overdue change?"

Suddenly she feels nervous, unsettled. "Change?"

Laura's laugh caresses her ears. "You do still want to be one of us, don't you, Kaarina?"

They all stare at her with equal gravity. Markus looks wide-eyed and slightly panicky. He reaches for Kaarina's arm, but Doctor Solomon blocks him and turns Kaarina toward the doorway.

"Let's get you some dry clothes, dear. If you'll kindly follow me. Once you're nice and dry, I have some thrilling news to share with you."

They start toward the door. When Markus tries to

follow them, the nurses block his way. The doctor turns and gives him a smile, wraps her arm around Kaarina's shoulders.

"Now Mister Nyman. Don't you worry about Kaarina here. She's in excellent hands. You had better run along, now. Being late wouldn't be the best thing for your social rank and I happen to know your supervisor Mattinen is a very punctual woman. You wouldn't want to risk that fabulous house of yours, just because you were a couple minutes late one morning, would you?"

The door shuts behind them, muffling Markus's reply.

The glass shakes slightly in her hands. Kaarina tightens her grip on it, staring at the miniature waves appearing on the surface of the water. It isn't easy to process the doctor's words.

They've done it.

They fixed it.

An Unchipped brain, successfully integrated with the city's CS. And she's next in line.

She takes another sip, then clears her throat. "And you're sure? The chip will definitely work this time?"

"My dear, I'm positive. We're already seeing excellent results from other test subjects in the facility."

"Test subjects?"

"My apologies, dear. I mean other Unchipped, here in the center."

Small wrinkles around the doctor's eyes, her blonde hair tied into a careless ponytail, and the loose-fitting college shirt under her white jacket make her seem so… *ordinary*.

And yet she's the mastermind behind fixing her chip—this process of making Kaarina normal. Someone who can eat, drive, walk, shop, and live in the city. No more outcasts, cold Milkcap stew, or black market. No more knives at her throat. She'll be just like everyone else, just as ordinary.

"Can I think about it? For a day or two?"

The doctor turns to face her. Just like she used to, Laura squeezes her hand, and nods toward a white curtain at the end of the office they're sitting in. "Of course you can, dear. Though I don't see what there is to think about." The doctor shrugs and wipes her hands on her white lab pants. "But meanwhile, I've got a robe and some comfy clothes in there. Go ahead and change. You're absolutely drenched."

Kaarina glances at the curtain. Her stomach twists unpleasantly. She wishes Bill would say something. *You know it's been at least twenty minutes since your last "It's a scam" rant. Should I be worried?*

"Go on, sweetheart. Once you've changed, I'll show you the test results and some brain scans. It's amazing work, really. If I do say so myself."

Kaarina sits on her chair, still hesitating and staring at the curtain. One of the nurses walks over and puts her hands on the chair, gestures for Kaarina to get up.

While she slowly treads toward the curtain, Kaarina taps for Bill, hoping that changing her clothes will give her enough time to have a conversation with him.

After she steps into the small changing area, the nurse gives her a quick smile and closes the curtain. She looks almost identical to Nurse Saarinen.

Kaarina takes off her hoodie, clears her throat. Though she's just had a drink, she suddenly feels parched.

Bill? Care to join in here? What do you think is going on?

Her jeans fall to the floor in a sodden heap.

Bill? Come on, I need you. Stop acting like you're on your period.

The "comfy clothes" are more like rough paper on her skin. She wraps the hospital robe around her body and stares at herself at the mirror. Maybe she was wrong. Maybe this is a time-capsule. And it's taken her back to the day of the chipping, when someone drilled a hole in her head. The same day when she woke up early just to hear that she was doomed to be different from everyone else. An underdog.

And now, her second chance has arrived. The nightly vegan meals. Her very own comfy gaming chair. She'll finally be able to read the billboards and walk on the blue tiles.

Markus doesn't need her. Not really. He's just bored with life. As soon as he gets his new house, new neighbors, and a beautiful view... would he really want to hang out with someone like her? A woods person? And Raino already got what he needed. Thanks to Kaarina, he now knows his son is alive and well. Everyone else at the pharmacy will have to find another PI to track down missing persons. They'll surely find another Unchipped con artist to scam them out of their CC's.

The doctor peeks in. "You about ready? Let's go to the lab. You're not going to believe all the exciting news we have for you. You must be absolutely tickled, huh? Come on now, Nurse Niemi and Nurse Penttilä are almost done with their shift, and I've already asked them to watch their overtime." Doctor Solomon's chuckle is soft, genuine.

Something feels off. Why is the room spinning?

Bill, should I go with her?

The curtain opens and four nurses walk in. Two of them grab her by one arm, two of them by the other. When she walks between them, Kaarina does her best to focus on their faces. It's not four nurses after all. It's only two.

No—now it's four nurses again.

Two nurses.

Now it's four.

Her stomach flips but she doesn't vomit. The water in her empty belly slushes around as they make their way into the lab. From there they keep going: through the small hallway, and into an operating room.

Metal instruments lie on a metal tray. A hospital bed

with paper sheets sways slowly in the middle of the room. A tinted-glass pod, big enough to fit two Kaarinas in it stands next to the bed with wheels. It looks comfy, like a cradle to crawl into. The four nurses hold onto her until she lies safely on the bed. Two nurses let go of her, then disappear as if into thin air.

"What. Did you. Give. Me."

The doctor is humming, a sound that reminds her of the blue tiles that snake around the city. Kaarina stares at the ceiling, where the vents seem to multiply in front of her eyes.

"Bill. Are you. There."

Doctor Solomon chuckles softly. "I'm afraid your telepathic little friend can't hear you, dear." Her footsteps approach and a friendly face fills Kaarina's blurry field of vision. "It probably wasn't your brightest idea to tell a stranger about your West-Land connection. People may not trust each other, but they sure do spill the beans to improve their social ranks."

Another paper sheet is placed over Kaarina's body. Somehow, she's lost her robe somewhere. Maybe it's hiding somewhere outside this room. With her mind. With Bill.

"Now, I would be lying if I didn't tell you I was a tad disappointed to learn about your shenanigans in the city. The reason we left you alone all this time and never came after you is that you haven't participated in any of the nonsense the other loose test subjects get up to. I can't tell you how many of them we catch almost on a weekly basis, lurking around the city with their black trash bags."

Her chuckle tickles Kaarina's ears, soothes her mind.

The doctor scoffs. "Some black market they have going on. Rotting meat in plastic bags."

She reaches for an object, plugs something into a socket by the hospital bed. The sound of clippers whirring somewhere behind Kaarina's head startles her, but she's unable to move her head, or her hands, or her body.

The doctor's hands work steadily on her head. Wisps of short blonde hair fall onto the floor. "Our guards can basically smell them before they see them. I'm not sure what the market is for rotting animal flesh in this city, but whoever is buying it must be well vaccinated. And I guess they all are. The healthcare we provide is exceptional."

Kaarina fights the heaviness in her eyelids, fights the shadows closing in at the edges of the room. Whatever it was that they slipped into her water, it's about to kick in with full force.

"People can be so ungrateful. All we really want is for everyone to have peace of mind, for them to lead a worry-free life."

"Like. Raino."

"Oh yes, just like your pharmacist friend. Bless his old heart. No pills or programs or realities can cure that man's mind. He'll always live in the past, in regret and sorrow. It's only natural for him to give in, to come here and live with the rest of the damaged individuals."

"He will. Die."

Her laughter is now sharper, more impatient than before. "No dear, not die. He'll be plugged into the CS, resting inside one of these wonderful machines." Laura taps the stasis capsule's open door. "He'll be out cold, like he's taking a very, very long nap. Just like you will be soon. You'll get a neat job, just like your friend Markus has at the Server-Center. The only difference is that you won't be going home at four o'clock in the afternoon."

The doctor's words jolt Kaarina into greater alertness. Her mind screams at her to run, to hide, to fight. There's no fixing the chip. No cure. No brain scans. Just a cord and her brain—to be forever used as a server for those living in the augmented reality.

The doctor lifts a syringe, pushes out a drop of liquid. A nurse wearing a white mask lifts Kaarina's hand and attaches it to an IV.

Solomon walks closer with a syringe in her hand. Whatever substance inside, it's about to find its way to Kaarina's veins, her body, her being. Will she be the same, when she next wakes up? Or someone else? Something else?

A loud *bang* stops her hands. The light in the operating room flickers, then goes out with a *zap*.

The doctor's chuckle sounds eerie in the dimly-lit room. The syringe clinks against the metal tray next to the operating table.

"Oh, Mister Nyman. Why didn't you just go to work like I told you to?"

The strangely soft and comfortable operating table caresses her body. The paper blanket on top of her may as well be a down comforter, or one of the cozy sleeping bags in the attic above the barn.

The ceiling light is out. No one's in the room with her. How long has it been since the nurses and the doctor ran off? Five minutes? Five hours? Longer?

One by one, her fingers reconnect with her brain. She fingers the paper sheets, feels their rough surface. Her shaved head feels like it weighs too much for her to sit up and look around. But it doesn't matter. There's nothing left there for her to see.

This is the end. No second chances for her. No more options to choose from. The city. The barn. Even joining the Unchipped. All of it is now out of her reach. She's doomed to be alone. Her mind turned off forever.

A dull voice is hollering again at the back of her mind, like it's coming from under water. Too tired to focus on anything else, she lets the strange comfort of the operating table lull her in.

How her head fits perfectly between the blocks that stop her from turning.

"Kay."

The thermostat's pleasant whirr.

"Kay-Kay, answer me."

The warm sensation under her bum and around her thighs.

"Wake the fuck up, Kay."

"Bill?"

"Yes it's me, you dim-wit. Snap out of it. Time to go."

"But I'm so comfy…"

"You're not comfy, you're the opposite of comfy. You're about to score a drill through your skull and you just pissed yourself. Get the fuck up. Let's move before the evil witch and her puppies come back. Chop chop!"

Slowly, she opens her eyes but doesn't move a muscle. With slurred words, she says, "Get up? Why? To run away? And where to, Bill?" She needs to take a breather before continuing. "I'll never be Chipped. I'll never live in the city."

"So go back to the woods, Kay. Do you really want to be one of these murderous fucks, anyway?"

"The Unchipped will kill me. Just like they were going to kill Rocky."

"Last I checked, the black market is not really big on human flesh. Now get up. You can moan and drown in self-pity later. Don't you want to make sure Ässä finds a new home before you let the crazy scientist plug you into that death-capsule? And make sure Rocky is okay?"

Kaarina lets her head press heavily against the operating table. "The dog's better off without me. And so is Rocky."

Bill stops talking. Has she won the debate? For the first time ever? Before she has time to celebrate, Bill's muffled voice returns.

"Okay, fine. I didn't want to pull this card. But it looks like your head is way too deep in your ass for me to do anything else. Remember when I agreed to help the old pharmacist? When I risked my life for you to score a few nasty vegan-bars?"

Her eyelids feel less dense. Raino's relieved laughter echoes through her tired brain.

"Yes, to help him. You said you'd owe me. Well, I've come to collect. Get. The Fuck. Up. Kay."

Pouting like a kid whose mother has just denied her five more minutes of sleep, she wiggles her toes, her feet, her legs. Her head and upper body heavy, she moves her right leg and lets it drop down from the table. Her body drags down, hangs halfway off her comfy prison. After moving her left leg off the table, she crashes down.

"That's okay, that's okay. You're off the bed. Now we need a door, let's find a way out of this torture chamber."

Still annoyed by Bill's interruption of her state of Zen, Kaarina gets on all fours and crawls toward the door. She cracks open the swinging door and takes a peek, scans the hallway. Doctor Solomon stands at the end of the corridor talking with two guards.

"They won't see you if you stay down. Keep going. There's a back door at the end of this aisle."

"How do you know that?" she whispers, but slips through the door and keeps going.

"I remember this hellhole from our previous visit. To your left and right, rooms for the Unchipped. At the end of

the aisle, the meeting room, kitchen, and the labs. The rest
of it we never saw."

A door at the end of the hall opens and two white
coats walk out. They stop to talk to one another, missing
her white hospital pajamas. Kaarina sits down and
presses her body against the wall, making herself as small
as she can.

A door opens next to her and a hand taps her
shoulder. She turns and sees a young girl with black
hair. It hangs long and covers most of her pale face. "In
here. Hurry," she whispers.

Kaarina glances back at the two doctors. They're
shaking hands, clearly at the end of their conversation.
They'll walk down the aisle and spot her soon.

Before she can think too much about it, she turns
toward the girl and lets her drag her into the room. The
door closes silently behind them.

The girl's round face forms a shy smile. Her widened
pupils have a hard time focusing. "Hi, I'm Sanna. I'm
Unchipped and have been here for three years now. Are
you new here? Have you just come from the operation?
What are you running away from?"

Reading the girl's face is hard because of the dark
hair hanging down in front of it. Kaarina fights the
sudden urge to reach for her face, to fix the locks of hair
behind her slightly pointy ears. She must be ten years
old, maybe younger.

"How is your door not locked?" Kaarina leans against
the door, as if trying to block anyone from entering.

"They trust me. Though I do have a secret. One that only scar-skulls are allowed to see."

"Scar-skulls?"

Sanna's eyes investigate Kaarina's skull and find a scar from a chipping procedure gone wrong. Clearly eager to reveal someone her secret, Sanna gestures Kaarina to follow her to a walk-in closet by the door. Kaarina manages to crawl a few inches before she collapses on the floor. Sanna slides open one of the closet doors. First, all Kaarina can see is a row of blue thermo-shoes. Then something small and round hops out the closet. A wide grin takes over Sanna's face.

"His name is Mister Bun-Bun."

Kaarina stares at the rabbit, now climbing onto Sanna's lap. The girl's gentle fingers stroke the critter's white and black fur.

"How on earth did you find a bunny in the Chip-Center? Was he at the lab?"

"I didn't find Mister Bun-Bun. I bought him. From the black market."

Was the rabbit supposed to be dead when Sanna bought it? Why would the Unchipped deliver live animals, and to a place like the Chip-Center, buzzing with guards?

"Does Laura know you have a bunny?"

Sanna shakes her head for no.

"But it's my only secret, I swear. Doctor Laura trusts me. She never goes through my things. I even get to go on tours with Doctor Laura. I've been told that if I'm good and do what I'm told, I'll be the first one to get chipped once they figure out what's wrong with me."

Kaarina can't fight the temptation anymore. She pushes the black hair aside. The shy smile on the girl's round face deepens. She's like a porcelain doll.

"There's nothing wrong with you, Sanna. You're just not plugged into their system, that's all. It doesn't make you invalid or less important. Do you talk to the others at all?"

Again, she shakes her head. "We're not allowed. You're the first person to ever meet Mister Bun-Bun."

Kaarina fights the urge to hug the girl. How has she managed, all alone, all these years? Just her and her bunny. Isolated, vulnerable. Hopeless. A product of the Chip-Center. Just one of Doctor Solomon's multiple victims.

Raino's face flashes through Kaarina's mind. "Sanna, do any old people ever come to the center? Or have any of the other test subjects ever gone missing?"

Sanna's eyes scan the ceiling as she processes Kaarina's question. "Yes, I've seen old men and women. One or two of them come in each week, I think. Some of the scar-skulls sometimes disappear. I help the nurses with their rounds. Each door has a small book with a scar-skull name and age. I check them all the time. I try to memorize the names. It's a game me and Mister Bun-Bun play."

"And you don't know where the missing scar-skulls are taken to?"

"Of course I know. They go to the basement. I get to see them sometimes. It's like a big aquarium. But instead of fish, there's a lot of naked people."

An image of a tinted glass stasis capsule flashes through Kaarina's mind. That's where she would be now, sleeping, turned off. That is if Markus hadn't stuck around and caused a scene. Kaarina imagines hundreds of stasis capsules hidden underground. Thousands. That must be where Doctor Solomon stacks people that don't fit in her agenda.

Kaarina takes the girl's hands, squeezes them tight. She hopes this gesture will make Sanna trust her, like the Chipped people did back in the city. "It's not an aquarium. It's a bad place, Sanna. This whole place is bad. They bring people in and turn them into computers. They'll never wake up. They'll be like vegetables. Do you understand what—"

A yell echoes from the hallway, followed by hurried footsteps.

"Leave the girl. You gotta go Kay. They've figured out you're missing."

Sanna nods at the door, then at Kaarina. "I think they're looking for you," she says and gives a little smile. "Can I see you again? Can you come back to see me and Mister Bun-Bun soon?"

Kaarina braces herself against the wall, tries to turn—and collapses to the floor.

"Again. Try again."

The drugs have worn off enough for her to hear Bill

again, but not enough to make her body obey her brain.

"Here, let me help…" Two little hands help Kaarina off the floor and walk her to a window with an airing vent. Sanna opens the vent and pulls out the grid. "You'll fit. The scar-skull who brought me Mister Bun-Bun did."

Kaarina sits on the window shelf, grabs her legs, one at a time, and shoves them through the gap in the window. Once she's out, she falls like an abandoned rag doll dropping off a table. Outside, she does her best to stand on her own two feet, as wobbly as they are. She turns back to face the girl on the other side of the window.

"Listen, I won't be coming back. But you can look for me. In your mind, just try and picture me and search for me…. It sounds crazy. But you'll see. You just need to skip your pills for one night. And you'll be able to talk to me again."

Sanna cocks her head a bit, stares at Kaarina with her wide round eyes. The sound of doors opening close by her room alarms her. Leaning forward she stage-whispers, "I'll do it tonight. I get it. It's like talking to a spirit or a ghost. I'll do what you said."

"No, that's not spiritual what I—"

The door to Sanna's room opens right after she closes the window. Somehow the girl has time to take a quick step to her gaming chair and throw herself on it. The AR-glasses back on her face, she looks like she's been watching cartoons all along. When a guard walks in, Kaarina ducks down.

"They'll continue their search outside any minute now. You got to run. Or crawl. I don't give a damn if you roll, just get out of there."

Her feet are shaky underneath her, but Kaarina takes off running anyway. At the corner of the building she trips on her own feet, falls flat on her face on the frozen ground. It's getting dark. Is it nighttime? How long has she been drugged for?

Lying flat against the cold ground, she hears someone yelling from the front yard. Two or three minutes, that's all she has until they'll circle the building and find her limp on the ground with mud in her mouth. She might as well let them. But it's either her promise to Bill, or a pure rush of adrenaline that keeps her fighting for one more successful escape from the Chip-Center.

"Check the side yard and the back." It's Doctor Solomon, calling out to the guards.

Thirty seconds. Twenty-nine. Twenty-eight.

A movement in the distance catches her eye. Across the rapeseed field, a man jumps up and down, waving his hands fiercely. He ducks back into the shadows of the trees, then jumps forward again waving, then disappears again behind the thick spruce tree.

"It's the blue-boy, Kay. Go to him!"

"Who?"

"Your first escort customer, what's his face... Mike? Mannie?"

Her eyes clear and lock on the frantically jumping man.

"Markus."

Just as the guard's footsteps get closer, about to turn the corner, Kaarina takes off running. Instead of trying to get out through the main entrance, she heads toward the stone wall.

Stumbling and tripping, she somehow makes her way to the wall. It's the same one where she once found a carving with a message she didn't take to heart, back when she still had the option to choose.

Without looking back, she jumps against the wall, placing her bare feet on the rough stones. Her fingers search for handholds. She's almost at the top.

"Do not look back, do not look back, do not look back…" The words tumble from her numb lips like a mantra.

Another shout pierces the crisp air. "Side yard all clear! Check the back!"

Her stomach now flat against the top of the wall, she slides her legs over and lets her body drop. This time the landing leaves her winded.

"Back is clear, no sign of the test subject!"

Her vision blurred, her mind and body fatigued, she stares at Markus's figure in the distance. An image of Sanna's straight black hair dances at the back of her mind. Random thoughts take over, making it impossible for her to focus on escape.

Why didn't the Unchipped kill Sanna's rabbit?

Does Bill always have strawberry margaritas and cheesecake for breakfast?

Why were there so many pills spread around mother's dead body, when the pill bottle never dropped from her cold hand?

"Hey, Kid?"

Her eyelids heavy, she looks up for a split second. Then she lets her forehead fall back into the frozen mud. Markus is nowhere to be seen. Perhaps he's gone, or perhaps he's only hiding behind the trees.

The hurried footsteps of the guards thud from the other side of the wall, along with heavy breathing and swearing. One of them stops only a meter or two away from Kaarina's resting body.

"Kid? You there? Some weird Yankee told me to tap for you. Said you'd pay well if I helped you out. He's a pain in the ass, won't leave me be. Where you at?"

The corner of her mouth twitches when she hears Yeti describing Bill. Bullseye.

"Kay-Kay, that's Yeti. He's coming for you. He'll help you out. But you need to wake up, now."

A small chuckle escapes her lips. "Yeti. And a Yankee. Sitting. In a tree..." she says, mumbling quietly.

"Kid? The Yankee says you're at a brain-drill center? Wait... Okay, and something about yellow dead flowers and a carved stone wall. Not sure if this lunatic is right in the head, but I'm almost at the Chip-Center, I assume that's where you are."

"That's what I just said to this Neanderthal, a Chip-Center!"

Their frantic voices muffled and distant at the back of her mind, Kaarina drifts off to the sound of retreating footsteps and faraway cries. Her body seems to flatten into the hard ground.

"Okay, Kid. Some blue-suited weirdo with a mop-top just showed me where you are. I'm coming to get you."

CHAPTER 5
BEYOND THE
COMFORT ZONE

Kaarina's head bounces against something hard. She slowly opens her eyes, finds that she's hanging upside down.

Moss, pine needles, rocks, mushrooms, and tree stumps flash before her eyes. Muffled but fierce barking fills her ears. When she manages to lift her head, Ässä's little terrier face greets her from a few feet away. The biggest combat boots she's ever seen take long strides along the forest path.

"Get! Get! You little shit…" Yeti's voice booms somewhere nearby. She's unsure if the man has spoken the words out loud or if he's still tapping her.

Ässä trots along but keeps his distance. The terrier is clearly wary of the strange man who is carrying his friend through the woods. He might turn around and try to launch a kick. It's possible he already has, but Ässä is a nimble little dog. Any attempt to boot him would probably have missed, making Ässä even more determined to harass the man carrying his friend.

Arms pushing against Yeti's wide and muscular back, Kaarina tries to free herself from his grip. "Okay, you can put me down now. I can walk from here."

Yeti's laughter rumbles through his upper body. Hands wrapped tight around Kaarina's legs, the man keeps his steady pace through the woods.

They pass a rock Kaarina recognizes. A scrap of silver tape still rests on the ground, next to Euros and other debris.

"I said, put me… down!"

Kaarina's fist strikes his lower spine, but there's no hint that it causes him any pain. He walks along without a word.

At her second punch, he stops.

After the third one, he lets go of her legs.

Kaarina falls to the hard ground.

Ässä stops barking as soon as he reaches Kaarina. A small wet snout investigates her face, licking and puffing. A sharp pain burns in her ribcage. She must have bruised something when she fell from the wall.

The Yeti leans against a tree and crosses his arms. After giving her a few seconds to lift her bruised body from the ground, his interrogation of her begins. "The Yankee said you'd have a black backpack with you, stuffed with goodies. Said that I could keep what's inside if I helped you out. Seems to me that we have a problem."

She crashes down on all fours, then sits down on the frozen path. Ässä jumps and circles around her bruised and exhausted body, his tail wagging wildly. Kaarina pets the dog halfheartedly. The pain in her chest worsens.

"And what kind of problem is that?"

His deep laughter sounds more amused than anything else. "Well, I don't see you carrying any bags and I'm pretty sure that hospital gown won't fit me."

"So what? Why'd you help me, then? You could see I didn't have a bag with me."

"So, I don't work for free. How are you going to pay for my rescue services?"

Face flushed dark pink, she makes two fists and stares at the Yeti's amused eyes. "Are you really going to stand there and give me that rapey shit again?"

Surprise flashes in his eyes and his grin widens. "What? I'm *rapey*?" He stands tall now, his humongous arms hanging long by his wide frame.

"Jesus this Moose is big. No wonder he's after your antibiotics. He must need the same dosage your horses do."

"Not now, Bill."

Her legs are still wobbly, and her upper body twitches with pain. She manages to stand for two seconds, just to crash back down on the ground.

The Yeti takes a step toward her. When Kaarina crawls onto her knees and raises her fists, he spreads his hands as if asking for a truce. "Easy now. I was just going to help you up." As she lowers her hands again to support her body, he walks over and grabs her by the shoulders. In what seems like a split second, she's standing upright, holding onto the Unchipped man who's come to her rescue.

He lets her hold onto his bicep while he continues with his questions. "You were talking to someone called Bill. Is that the Yankee?"

"Don't let that beefcake call me that."

"Yeah, that's him. You can just keep calling him a Yankee."

"Oh that's nice, Kay. Real classy. And you're welcome by the way. That's the last time I'm going to be saving your ungrateful ass."

She lets go of Yeti's arm to stand uncertainly on her own feet. A careful step—an attempt to walk—sends a riot of pain through her ribcage.

"Listen, I just want to go home and stuff my face with whatever moldy breadcrumbs I can find. Forget that this nightmare ever happened. I'll never visit the city again. Your suburbs and your food don't interest me. I'd much rather starve to death than see anyone, with or without a chip, ever again. And you can go. I don't need a babysitter. Just come by tomorrow and I'll pay—"

Her voice fades out as the street lights down by the tree line all die at once. The familiar hum is abruptly silent. The utility poles are dead.

"Did they just..." she takes a careful step, then another. The panic about to take control of her makes it easier for her to ignore the pain.

"Holy shit. Shit shit shit, Kid! What have you done?"

"They cut the electricity?"

The Yeti focuses on whoever talks inside his head. "The suburbs are dark too, including the camp. Some of my guys are heading out to see why, but I bet you already know the answer to that question. What the actual fuck happened in there? Why did you run?"

"They tried to drill into my brain and turn me off."

He just stares at her for a moment like he doesn't understand what she's saying. "You need to be more specific than that," he says. She feels compelled to continue.

"They turn off old people too. Store them away."

"They kidnap them?"

"I don't know! I mean, have any of your people ever gone missing?"

The horror in his eyes is the only answer she needs.

"Yeah, I bet that's where they are. At the Chip-Center," she continues, shaking her head, rush of horror taking her over. "She promised me she could fix my chip. That's why I went in…If Markus hadn't been with me—"

"Who is this *she?*"

"Laura… Doctor Solomon. She said they can turn Unchipped into Chipped. That's when they drugged me. Next thing I knew I was lying on an operating table, staring at a drill."

The Yeti shakes his head. Not a trace of amusement

remains on his face. "What kind of an assbrain trusts anything the Chipped have to say? And why the hell would you even consider becoming one of them? To live in some make-believe world, staring at things that don't exist for the rest of your life? As far as I can tell, whenever I have to visit the city, those suckers seem depressed as fuck. I would chop my hands off before I'd ever let them get their filthy hands on my brain again."

Shame washes over her. Why *did* she want to become Chipped so badly? After everything she had already seen in the city?

Raino, giving up on life, full of regret and sorrow.

The blue suits at the pharmacy, desperately seeking comfort from things like rabbit feet and happiness pills.

Markus, lonely and tormented by a promise of materialism.

How would her life be any better if she was Chipped? She'd be drugged every night, brainwashed to work for things she doesn't really need. Then she'd be drugged some more, so her numb brain could manage to believe she's happy and content with life.

"I'm not going to say I told you so."

After ignoring Bill and turning her face away from the Yeti's stern stare, Kaarina takes another shot at walking. The power being shut down means war. A whole new kind of witch hunt. She needs to get back to the barn. Find a weapon. No matter what her old morals and rules say about it.

Three steps forward. She stumbles on a rock, falls

face down on the pine needles that cover the path.

"Just let me carry you to the barn."

"No. Don't touch me."

She tries to shoo him away, but the Yeti dodges her hand. "Stop that. Just let me get you up before—"

"Back off. I don't need your help."

He huffs but stands still, watching Kaarina crawl slowly forward on the path. "Clearly."

His comment gets through to her. She lets her body fall limp on the forest floor. "Even if I would be willing to accept your help… I lied. I don't have anything at the barn to pay you with. You should go back to your people and hide until the guards are back in the city and the power's turned on again."

This gets his attention. In two long strides, he's by her side. Like he's picking up a ragdoll, he lifts her up and holds her steady. "What if the power *doesn't* come back on? How are we supposed to live in the suburbs without electricity? We'll freeze to death."

Unsure what to tell him, she stares into his startled eyes, wondering why she was once so intimidated by this man. Sure, he's big and strong, kind of a creep. Yes, he's the leader of a black market gang… but suddenly it seems unlikely that this man would ever hurt her.

"Wait!"

The shout carries through the woods. The Yeti suddenly shoves her back behind him. Embarrassed to touch him but without much of a choice, Kaarina holds onto the man by his waist. Even with his support, her legs shake and totter beneath her weight.

"Oh, it's this doofus again."

Markus's blue suit flickers between the pine trees, as he runs toward them—two black backpacks swinging from his back.

The Yeti walks in circles around the dimly lit barnyard. A flashlight beam shines on the gravel, bouncing around in the man's grip. He's in the middle of a conversation with the rest of his gang, his mouth pressed into a hard, stern line.

Kaarina rummages through her things up in the hayloft. She packs what she can fit in the new backpack Markus handed her in the woods. The Yeti hasn't claimed it—at least not yet. She zips it up, then stares off into space for a moment. Where she's about to go next, she has no idea.

Rocky's nowhere to be seen, which makes her happy and relieved. Now healthy and strong, the gelding has rejoined the herd that roams around in the nearby woods. The horses will look for her to check for food. They'll be confused when they don't find any, but they won't starve without her here. There is plenty of food around for them to eat—hay, grass, and plants. These days the winters are too short to kill it all off. They'll learn to survive without human help.

A careful knock on the door draws her attention. Markus walks in, wearing a black and purple women's winter jacket and matching snow pants. He spreads his hands and laughs a little. "Got a matching knit hat to go with this?" It's weird to see him without a blue suit on.

The Yeti's voice rumbles from the barnyard. "Okay you two, quit your crossdressing and come downstairs. I've talked to my people. At least a dozen Chipped are making their way through the woods. They're definitely coming for you, Kid."

She grabs her bag and flashlight, points the light beam down the hayloft stairs that lead them back down to the barnyard.

The Yeti has fallen silent again by the time they get to him. He stands still, staring into nothingness. Then he nods and brings his focus back to this place and moment. Kaarina reads his expression: calm, cool, collected. Why wouldn't he be? He doesn't care what happens to her, whether she's dragged back onto that operating table or not.

But he also hasn't tried to steal her black backpack, or anything else of hers. He seems uninterested in the animals around the barn, except Ässä whom he must shoo away every other minute. The dog has changed his opinion about the big man. The terrier now eagerly jumps against his leg, doing all he can to get the Yeti's attention.

The Unchipped leader hasn't harmed any of them in any way. Instead, he's offered his help.

Maybe the power being cut off has made him nervous, unsure of what's to come.

Markus breaks the silence. "A dozen guards. That can't be good." He hugs his own black backpack against his chest, shivering in the cold night air. The blue suit he has abandoned up in the hayloft, behind the bales and old IKEA storage boxes, must have had a hell of a thermo-system.

"It's not guards."

Two beams of light shine on Yeti's face.

"What do you mean? Is it the nurses? The city employees?"

When the man grunts and covers his eyes, Kaarina stops dazzling him with the flashlight and overwhelming him with her questions. Markus's light remains stubbornly fixed on the scarred face.

"I'll tell you if you stop burning my eyes out with that damn thing."

Markus's flashlight turns off. "Is it the doctors? The Server-Center management?"

The Yeti walks up to Markus and stops—a few inches too close. Markus stops asking questions. This man is twice his size. Before Markus has time to react, the man grabs his flashlight and starts back toward the woods.

"No, you mop-headed fool. It's the blue suits. Looks like they sent the sheep to do their dirty work."

The Unchipped community, the people Kaarina used to despise, now remind her of a colony of ants. Their shapes move in the night from one house to another.

Yeti's people took her in without questions. They gave Markus hot tea, handed her a thicker coat and a pair of winter gloves. They seem nice. Friendly. Caring. Has she been wrong about them? All this time?

Some of them gather around the Yeti, like they're there to watch his back. Kaarina recognizes some of their faces from their last visit to her barnyard. So they're—what—the Yeti's soldiers? His bodyguards?

A woman with eyes cold and hard like glass steps closer. She, whom Kaarina once nicknamed Glass-Eye, leans in and whispers in her ear. "What gives, girl? Suddenly you're no better than us?" Glass-Eye nods at Yeti. "Now that you need his protection?"

Kaarina stares forward, unsure what to say. "I just didn't want the animals to die," she then mumbles.

"You'd rather have us die instead?" The woman glances at her leader and lowers her voice. "Do you even know what the black market meat gets us? Because I do. Antibiotics. Painkillers. Vitamins. Fresh vegetables. We don't kill just for the sake of killing. We kill only if we have to. To survive."

An image of a young, black-haired girl holding a black and white bunny flashes through Kaarina's mind. Suddenly she knows who smuggles pets inside the Chip-Center. Who crawled through the same window that helped Kaarina to escape.

Kaarina turns to face the Unchipped woman. When Glass-Eye sees her eyes, teary and regretful, she waves Kaarina off.

"Save your tears, girl. Just forget it. We got bigger rabbits to fry."

Glowing red, the tiki torches light up the yard. The Unchipped leader's enormous shadow covers a third of the old playground Kaarina and Markus are standing in. Slides, sandboxes and swing sets make the giant leader look like something out of this world—indestructible and god-like.

Would this creature stand against an army of the Chipped?

Shifting her weight from one foot to another, Kaarina stands next to the Yeti. Markus hovers behind the odd pair. Heartbeats thump inside Kaarina's head, but she's unsure who they belong to. They're all tapping one another. All listening in.

She closes her eyes and hopes that no one catches her talking to her distant friend. Or is Bill even that much of a secret at this point? Now that the Yeti knows about him? Now that Markus knows?

I don't want them to get hurt, Bill. They're innocent people. She's not entirely sure who her thoughts are referring to: those with the chip or those without.

In her mind's eye, Kaarina sees Bill shrug before he replies. *"At least they're not carrying guns. You'll have a better shot dodging a knife than a bullet."*

From the corner of his eye, the Yeti glances at her. Then he quickly refocuses on the conversation going on inside his own head. Lips pressed into a hard line, Kaarina continues her conversation with Bill.

Why blue-suits, Bill? Why would they leave their lazy-boys, AR-movies, and government paid nightly highs, just to hunt down a nobody—a hobo that lives in the woods?

"Maybe they're being forced to. Or maybe something has changed."

People don't change, Bill. People hate change.

Rubbing her temples, Kaarina closes her eyes and hopes that she's wrong, and Bill is right. Then, a movement in the distance catches her eye. Something hovers by the tree line, right outside the playground. As she counts the hovering silhouettes in her head, Kaarina fails to answer Bill silently. "I guess we're about to found out."

The Chipped arrive in pairs. One by one, their dark blue shapes move against the tree line surrounding the playground. They've come for Kaarina. To drag her back into the city and onto that operating table. To make her leave her new-found allies behind. No more Ässä, Rocky, or Markus. She'll be removed from their world, this reality.

But maybe it's not just her who the blue suits are collecting? Maybe it's all of them?

As she stands here, side by side with all these people, what she has done is suddenly more apparent to her than it's ever been. She has started a war. Not intentionally, but still. Maybe she belongs in that death-capsule. If she was now turned off and forgotten, these people wouldn't be in danger. There'd be no war. The power would pop back up. The Unchipped community would be allowed to stay in the suburbs. Markus would keep his job and move into his luxury house.

Everything would remain the same, except that Doctor Solomon would have a new fish in her aquarium.

But she knows how fragile it is—her wish for a better life for those who now stand beside her. Because Doctor Solomon will come for them. All of them. Kaarina is not the cause of this war, only the catalyst. She's just a small piece in a big puzzle that they're all part of.

No one says a word. Not a whisper breaks the silence around them. Only footsteps on the frosty ground, and Ässä's low crawl by Kaarina's side.

More dark figures appear from the woods. They gather silently around the playground, not stepping in past its low log fence but lining up alongside it. Their blue thermo-shoes seem rooted to the ground beneath the slowly falling snow.

There are twenty or thirty of them… maybe more.

Markus moves closer, positions himself between the Yeti and Kaarina. He opens his fists, then closes them again. Is he second-guessing his decision? It's not too late for him to tell the other blue suits that he was kidnapped. Dressed in women's clothing against his will. Too terrified to run away, but dying to get back to his nightly tea, AR-glasses, and happiness-pills, all waiting for his return back in the city.

The Yeti grinds his teeth with a low growl. The sound breaks the uncanny, nervous silence, then gets louder as more muffled footsteps appear at the edge of the playground. Five more pairs of thermo-shoes join the group outside the fence. The Chipped stand tall, staring at the Unchipped inside the playground.

Kaarina wishes Bill would say something. That he'd crack a joke to lighten her nervous mood. She senses him there, tapping, watching. For the first time she can remember, Bill seems speechless.

She wishes for one of the horses to neigh.

For a wolf to howl.

For a rooster to crow.

But she's not home at the barn anymore. She's joined the Unchipped. And she's brought the enemy right to her new allies' doorstep.

One of the blue suits steps forward. "We're looking for Miss Kaarina," he says. The tiki torch next to him shines a warm light on his face—a face Kaarina vaguely recognizes.

From behind him, another blue suit steps into the soft red light. This face she recognizes instantly: the young man at Raino's pharmacy, the one who lost his football team in a mass-suicide. Doctor Solomon has picked well. She's sent the kind-hearted, the trusting. They're here to do her dirty work.

Kaarina takes a wobbly step closer. "That's me, I'm Kaarina. I know you've come to take me to the city, and I'll come in peace. Just let the others be. They've got nothing to do with this."

Yeti and Markus move forward quickly to stand at her side. She doesn't need to look at the Unchipped leader to know he's rolling his eyes.

"What are you, a complete dimwit? Like I'm ever going to let them take you back, Kid. Like it or not, you're one of us now."

A snowflake lands on Kaarina's cheek, biting the sensitive skin around her scar. It wasn't the Yeti who carved this marking on her skin, but the man who came before him. What rules is the new leader breaking, by protecting someone who has first refused to be part of the Unchipped community, and then started a war with the city?

Another snowflake lands on her long eyelashes. Maybe it's snowing in the city as well. Maybe the Chipped are waking up to the charade that is their life. Maybe the artificial happiness is being exposed for what it really is. AR-glasses drop to the floor. Happiness-pills scatter all over the abandoned apartments and houses. Minds clear from their drug-induced state, suddenly awakened.

Maybe they're done binge-watching the wellness channels. Tired of devouring veggie-nuggets dripping in grease. Uncomfortable in their blue overalls that mold into oversized gaming chairs.

But she knows better: it never snows in the city. If it does, the snowflakes are there to see, not to feel. Frostbite will never stand a chance—not where the Chipped live.

A woman in blue walks forward. She stops by the sand box a few feet away. Kaarina recognizes her immediately: she's the one who tells knock-knock jokes. "We're not here to take you back. We're here to join you."

"It's a scam."

"Shut up, Bill." The Yeti and Kaarina speak the words at the exact same time. The woman with the knock-knock jokes frowns at their odd choice of words but doesn't say anything.

"They're here to slice and dice you. With blue bread knives hidden in their ridiculous thermo-suits."

Kaarina's heart pounds wildly against her chest. "Why would you want to leave the city? It's cold out here, snow and ice all over. We have no power now. No shows or health care or proper food."

The snowflakes get thicker, icy against Kaarina's face. Markus reaches for her hand, squeezes it tight. Though his gesture feels odd, something out of this world, Kaarina lets him hold her hand. The Yeti rolls his eyes again.

"Getting laid all you two can think of?" His low voice rumbles through her head.

"Don't judge our Kay-Kay, man. It's been awhile. Who knows, maybe a good shag will turn that god-awful frown of hers upside down."

It's Kaarina's turn to roll her eyes. *I'm so glad you two wise-asses haven't lost your sense of humor. But it's not really a good time for a group-chat. How do we know these people are not here to harm us? Or spy on us?*

Their group-chat falls silent.

More blue suits move closer. Markus' hand squeezes tighter. Bill and the Yeti are holding their breath. She can hear their hearts beating.

An old, hunchbacked man appears from the crowd. Raino's arm is wrapped around a young girl with long, black hair. As they move closer, the girl smiles and nods shyly at Kaarina. A tiny black and white head with pointy ears pokes out from the girl's overalls' chest pocket. A voice Kaarina's never heard before—not inside her head—soothes her mind.

"Look at all the scar-skulls, Kaarina. I don't have to hide Mister Bun-Bun anymore."

Raino and Sanna stand so close to Kaarina that she can hear the old man breathe heavily. In their native language, he speaks slowly. *"On aika jättää laatikko taakse. Ja palata oikeaan maailmaan."*

Staring at the old man, the Unchipped process his words. Kaarina investigates his face, his half-blind eyes. Not a trace of dishonesty there to be found.

"Raino, you do understand that we need to run? That I've started a war?"

The old man reaches for Kaarina's shoulder. "I understand. We all do."

A careful smile lights up her face. The Yeti stares at the old man, gives him a nod. Finally, the Unchipped leader steps aside and turns to talk with his people. Markus also smiles and nods, then heads over to greet the blue suits he recognizes. Some of them hug each other. A ripple of chuckles and laughter cuts the crisp night air.

"Excuse me? Don't leave a Yankee hanging. What did the grandpa say?"

Kaarina hugs Raino and then lets the man follow in Markus's footsteps back into the blue crowd. She wraps her arm around Sanna and gives her a squeeze, careful not to scrunch Mister Bun-Bun. The girl giggles happily. A number of the Unchipped walk out of the houses, carrying clothing, packages of crispbread and bottled water.

She looks down at her warm and sturdy winter boots, the ones the Chipped gave her back at the pharmacy. No duct tape, no rips, or tears appear on their black surface. She moves her fingers inside the comfy gloves that the Unchipped gifted her, as soon as she had entered the playground and their lives.

Warm. Dry. Not alone. How did she end up here, among allies and friends?

"Hello? You know I don't speak Swedish, Kay. What did the old guy say?"

Kaarina lifts her chin and gazes up at the night sky. Snowflakes continue to melt against her face but now the sensation is pleasant. Friendly chatting fills the playground while people introduce themselves.

Jaana. Hannu. Kimmo. Raino. Niina. Mikko. Joonatan. Vilja... She'll make sure to learn their names, and hopefully their life stories as well. Not because it'll help her to survive and run away from Doctor Solomon. Not because it's the right thing to do. She'll get to know these people, Chipped and Unchipped. Because together, they'll be stronger. Happier.

"Kay-Kay, I swear—"

"Okay, okay, Bill. I just needed a minute. I haven't forgotten you. How could anyone ever forget about you when you're such a pain in the ass?" Her smile gives her away. Above all, Kaarina's most grateful for the chatty Californian that lives inside her head. The one that has stayed by her side all these years. Even at times when she didn't deserve it.

"Yeah, yeah, yeah. Love you too, Kay-Kay. What did the old man say?"

"He said they're done living in a box. That it's time to return."

"Return where?"

"Into the real world."

EPILOGUE

"Why don't you come back to bed? You've been sulking out here in the dark for hours."

William doesn't need to turn around to know that Miguel is leaning on the doorframe, his dark figure wrapped in a fluffy white robe. If he turned around, he'd see Miguel's eyes drilling into him, muscular arms crossed on his chest, one foot folded behind his fit figure to press against the open balcony door.

Instead of looking at Miguel, Bill stares at the silhouette of the mountains, rising all around them. In the middle of the enormous valley sleeps City of California. The mansion is built high enough on the mountain side for them to see the neon-green glow of the tiles, billboards, and buildings. Right now, the reflection is barely visible. It's four a.m.. The Chipped will be dozing under the influence of their mandatory sleeping pills for three more hours.

"You're not going to hear from her until the morning. I'm sure she's okay. And there's nothing you can do anyway."

"It's midday in City of Finland. She's not answering my tapping. Something's going on."

Miguel sighs, walks across the balcony, and leans his arms against the cool metal railing. "She's a grown woman, Bill. Not some hormone-driven, brainless teenager. I'm sure she'll let you in once the time is right."

"I don't trust that moose she travels with. The Unchipped are so fucking different over there."

"Different how?"

"It's all so morbid. And dark. All the freaking time. They basically don't have a pot to piss in. Who wouldn't lose their minds in that kind of a place?"

"And the moose she travels with?"

"Like a rabid animal. Victim of his caveman instincts and shit."

Miguel turns his head to hide his amusement. "Reminds me of someone we both know…"

"Whatever, Micky. Go back inside and pound sand. Up your ass."

A *clink* sounds from downstairs and Miguel leans over the railing. His upper body hanging over the metal edge, he taps whoever is tiptoeing downstairs right underneath them. His voice cuts the silence. "Eat that last slice of cheesecake, Arturo, and I'll skin you alive, make a purse, sell it on the black market, and feed what's left to the coyotes."

The kitchen light turns off. The only sound remaining is the sound of the crickets. Their chirping is a constant now. Long gone is the winter, and the feeling of crisp air caressing his skin after the sun goes down. Southern California is unbearably hot these days. And not just because of the wildfires.

Miguel's feet pat softly against the balcony tiles. Before he goes back inside, he turns around and says, "A new trailer arrived today. Parked by the orange trees, at the southeast edge of the farm."

Bill curses under his breath but doesn't turn around to face Miguel. "Of course it did."

"Should I send Maria or Phil to take care of it?"

"No, I'll do it."

Miguel scoffs loudly. "You? When's the last time *you* held a gun?"

"I said I'll take care of it. I'll go out there tomorrow or the day after."

"And meanwhile?"

"Let them be. Who the fuck cares? They'll eat, what, a few oranges and an avocado a day? Besides, taking care of them is like playing with a boomerang."

He can almost hear Miguel frown behind him.

"They'll just keep coming, Micky. Jesus on a bike! Go eat your granola or watch a chick-flick or something. Leave me alone."

But he stays, leaning against the white silk curtains that dance slowly in the night air.

"Stop shaking your stupid head at me."

"I'm not."

Don't lie to me, I can see you do it.

"Can you also see how you've grown soft in your old age?"

You are so full of shit that no wonder your eyes are brown. No, I have not grown soft in my old age. No, I'm not too preoccupied by "that Finnish chick" to take care of my own land. I said, I'll take care of it.

Miguel's laugh is light, amused. "No need to tap me when I'm standing ten feet away. And excuse me for being worried. But since when has it been okay by you to have freeloaders on the premises?"

A shrug is the only answer Miguel gets. Bill digs around in the pocket of his robe. He lights a hand-rolled cigarette, crosses his arms against the railing, and says, "And if you think I'm old, fuck you and the horse you rode in on."

Shoot! Book one of the Unchipped story is at a close. But don't worry, you can find out what happens next in Book 2 in the Unchipped series, UNCHIPPED: WILLIAM available on Amazon

My dearest reader,

You are simply amazing! Thank you so much for your support and readership! I can't tell you how much you reading this book means to me. I'm humbled and honored that you've dedicated your valuable time to experience the Unchipped universe with me. I'm still a newbie author, so if you were to leave me a review on Amazon it would be a huge help! Short or long, doesn't matter. Reviews are the best way to help other readers find the Unchipped Series.

Want to stay in touch? I would love it if you'd subscribe to my newsletter @ www.TayaDeVere.com/HappinessProgram Starting in August 2020, newsletter subscribers will receive free, exclusive early access to in-universe short stories from the Unchipped series a week before each book comes out. That's every eighteen days so be sure to sign up to get first crack at the series!

You can also find me on:

Facebook – facebook.com/tayadevereauthor
Instagram – instagram.com/tayadevere_author
Goodreads – goodreads.com/tayadevere
Bookbub – bookbub.com/authors/taya-devere
Amazon – amazon.com/Taya-DeVere/e/B07KRJPMTV

Gratefully yours,
Taya DeVere

THE END

About the Author

Taya is a Finnish-American author, writing contemporary fiction and dystopian sci-fi. After living and traveling in America for seven years, she now lives in Finland with her husband Chris, their dog Seamus, three bunny-boys (Ronin, Baby, Loki), and her horse of a lifetime, Arabella.

Best things in life: friends & family, memories made, and mistakes to learn from. Taya also loves licorice ice cream, second hand clothes and things, bunny sneezes, salmiakki, and sauna.

Dislikes: clowns, the Muppets, Moomin trolls, dolls (especially porcelain dolls), human size mascots and celery.

Taya's writing is inspired by the works of authors like Margaret Atwood, Peter Heller, Hugh Howey, and C.M. Martens.

Final Thanks

Writing this series is the best high. Getting to know my characters has sucked me into this universe, surprising me (and sometimes freaking me out), time and time again. Some nights I forget to go to bed. Some days I realize I haven't had anything to eat since my morning bowl of cereal-granola. The story takes a life of its own while I sleep, often waking me up in the middle of the night, forcing me to fill my phone's notebook with restless gibberish.

I want to thank my partner-in-everything Chris, for being my rock. Thank you for keeping me caffeinated. Thank you for your unwavering support, and for giving these books your hundred and ten percent. Also, thank you for knowing when it's safe to roll your eyes at me and to tell me what a ding-dong I am. Your belief in me kicks my writer's doubt's a** every single day.

Thank you, Chris T. and Lindsay, for your uncanny editing talent and genuine kindness. I'm so lucky and grateful to have you in my corner.

Last but not least, thank you, Luna and Piritta, for your out-of-this-world friendship. You two see through my BS, ground me when I'm unhinged, and love me for who I am. I love you both, from the bottom of my muddled heart.

The Unchipped series – Release schedule 2020
UNCHIPPED: KAARINA - 8/31/2020
UNCHIPPED: WILLIAM - 9/18/2020
UNCHIPPED: ENYD - 10/6/2020
UNCHIPPED: LUNA - 10/24/2020
UNCHIPPED: THE RESORT - 11/11/2020
~~UN~~CHIPPED: LAURA - 11/30/2020
~~UN~~CHIPPED: DENNIS - 12/18/2020